Andrea Nicole Elizabeth Hinth,

"To a teacher of life and
therfore a joy!"

stated by your
Uncle Frank

"Pierce Hubbard gage"

Kate Konow
Katherine Pierce Konow

katherinehoveman@yahoo.com

PIERCE HUBBARD GAGE

Love & Fury

a Medieval Masquerade

WestBow
PRESS

A DIVISION OF THOMAS NELSON

WestBow Press books may be ordered through booksellers or by contacting:

WestBow Press
A Division of Thomas Nelson
1663 Liberty Drive
Bloomington, IN 47403
www.westbowpress.com
1-(866) 928-1240

Because of the dynamic nature of the Internet, any web addresses or links contained in this book may have changed since publication and may no longer be valid. The views expressed in this work are solely those of the author and do not necessarily reflect the views of the publisher, and the publisher hereby disclaims any responsibility for them.

Any people depicted in stock imagery provided by Thinkstock are models, and such images are being used for illustrative purposes only.

Certain stock imagery © Thinkstock.

ISBN: 978-1-4497-7298-7 (e)
ISBN: 978-1-4497-7296-3 (sc)
ISBN: 978-1-4497-7297-0 (hc)

Library of Congress Control Number: 2012920601

Printed in the United States of America

WestBow Press rev. date: 11/06/2012

Contents

This book is dedicated to *love.*
– Pierce Hubbard Gage

Chapter I:

The Kidnapping

Once upon a time, in the days of knights, castles, and fire-breathing dragons, there lived a beautiful, fair young maiden named Cassandra.

She was a peasant girl or serf, as they were often called by the lord of the kingdom. Cassandra was in her sixteenth year when her kingdom Heartland was invaded by the evil knights of Rogenshire.

It happened at early dawn, when all the serfs left their huts to work out in the fields.

"Don't forget your bread and goat cheese, daughter," Cassandra's father shouted with a chaffed and aged throat. "Is Tirzah going to meet you when we sup tonight?" he asked with a hopeful voice.

"She's coming down to meet me this morning, Father."

"She can't do that!" he protested, coming up from behind her as she looked into an antiquated, cracked mirror inside a tarnished, silver-handled frame that Tirzah had given her. He pulled some straw out of the back of Cassandra's beautiful, long blond hair, put his other hand on her shoulder, and whispered firmly but softly in her ear, as if she were still a child, "What if Lord Wanton checks on our work and it is not done enough for him?" His voice quaked with worried fear.

"Okay," he said to himself, shifting his weight from her after he received no response, "don't think of your own back and its belting, but for God's sake, think of somebody else's ... and this prince! Oh Cassandra, Cassandra – "

"Father," Cassandra interrupted as she turned to look at him squarely in the eyes, "the prince has spoken to our overseer, Lord Wanton; he will say nothing today."

Cassandra's demeanor then changed, and she gazed at her father with a loving stare of seemingly gracious foreknowledge. She then winked as quickly as a hummingbird's wing and flicked her hair as she turned her head in fast focus toward her day's planned events. As she walked out of the hut, her poor father limped behind her, grabbed his walking stick, and shouted another protest, "I don't mind your precious friend Tirzah and you learning to read, but do it at night when we have a few minutes of our own time!"

Cassandra was almost thirty paces ahead of him, joining a group of serfs walking along a field path. The distance between the elderly father and the determined daughter had grown fast. She shouted back as she saw Tirzah waiting for her up ahead by the weeping willow tree along the same path, "I'm too exhausted at night from work; I can't see and neither can she because there is not enough light, and she has a hard time getting back into the shelter of the castle wall. They won't let the gate down for her!"

"Why not?" shouted the father.

"Because they make it hard for her, Father," shouted Cassandra, who was already forty paces ahead and counting.

"Because she is Jewish." The father finished the long-distance conversation as he suddenly fell in a slump on his stick in the dust of the path. He was trying hard to breathe; his chest was heavy and his soul worn-out by the world's savage work. He whispered his thoughts out loud to the leaves and the dust, "She gives to others and what do they do in return?" He moaned. "Stupid fools." He muttered this last thought in the lonesome morning chill that no one heard because all the serfs were now way ahead of him.

He did not know how much longer he could take this life, and his poor Cassandra was so brilliant in every way. Her fantasies of marrying this prince were something he did not even have the heart to discourage. He knew the prince had a real love for her, too, but the whole idea was ridiculous. The realities of this world had belted this poor peasant too many times, and yet, as he looked up toward the field, one more belt was about to strike him.

The great moat and castle wall were at least five hundred paces behind the elderly serf as the sun still rose; the knights, earls, dukes, and their ladies of the court were all fast asleep as their house servants made morning preparations within the protection of the wall. The nobility had gathered at Heartland for the prince's twenty-fifth birthday celebration. They were told this was a feast of two weeks in length. Their extra sleep was all part of the preparation to give them added energy for the exciting and exhilarating festivities of feasts and jousts and games galore.

A very tall, handsome, and regal man with shoulder-length, graying black hair, moustache, and goatee leaned a bit over the top of the great barricade, eating an apple for an early breakfast. Jacob Santoro, a merchant of Jewish heritage, had a large four-kingdom territory to cover selling silk cloth and rugs from the Far East. He had traded for more than twenty years along the old Roman roads of Christendom, with buying connections as far away as Venice and Constantinople. His one and only daughter Tirzah was the only family who dared to travel with him. On this western route, which he took yearly, he educated her in the mapping of the roads and the stars, mathematics, languages, and alchemy. His extended Venetian family could never seem to keep him in the city for more than two months at a time. "I have to make a living for all of us!" was always his reply to them. Jacob knew it was only half true. His family by now was well established and successful; he had a home in Venice but chose this harsher life willingly. At some point, Jacob would have to make some changes, but as a man caught between other people's conflicts and prejudices, he was forced to wait for a right moment. That moment was about to come.

Jacob watched Tirzah meet her pupil under the willow. The naval monocular he obtained from a very inventive Arab friend, a sea trader in Sicily, had proven very useful on land; it helped him avoid road robbers and find different exits through forests along various kingdoms to shorten travel time. He now used it to watch his daughter.

"My daughter is just like me," Jacob mused. "She picks both the peasants and the nobles to befriend." He chuckled to himself. "What is noble and what is peasant ..." His thoughts meandered through the valleys of his mind as he watched his daughter walk on with Cassandra. He thought about the old hermits and hags he met on his travels and the sundry outcasts in the various forests with whom he exchanged food and goods for precarious lodgings in between the inns of walled kingdoms and their majestic gentry longing for news from distant lands while buying cloth, carpets, and culture. These odd, simple folk eked out a forest living because they no longer wished to be slaves of the system and die under the boot of another man.

"Dear Lord, I can hardly blame them," Jacob said, interrupting his thoughts. "Most don't get a chance to be educated. Some have betrayed me to robbers while others have hidden me with Tirzah and all our goods inside their scant dwellings." He mused and resolved, "It must be every man's heart that rules the man, but how long can this kind of life I live last?"

Suddenly, Jacob saw that the old serf under the willow had started to scream uncontrollably on his knees.

With his monocular, Jacob observed with a chill, still frozen from the underworld, his worst foreboding nightmare come to life.

The awful, evil knights of Rogenshire galloped through the forest in perfect timing, intimidating the serfs with swords in hand. They placed their horses in between the field and the path to allow no escape to the castle. The serfs were too far away by now; the rogues just had their pick. With their swords they sliced, maimed, and killed any man trying to protect the women and rampaged the field until all was ruined.

After their hellish morning lark, the brutes from Rogenshire took away nine young damsels, and both Tirzah and Cassandra were included in their pilfering and kidnapping.

Chapter 2:

False Accusations and the Gauntlet

The old wailing serf under the weeping willow was overtaken and left in a sea of dust as newly awakened Heartland knights rode out to the rescue but to no avail. The forest had hidden the surprise kidnappers' entry from the Heartland lookout in the highest tower. After they made their final mocking "joust" with the last peasant man armed with a hoe, the rough reprobates rode away with screaming damsels through the same forest path from whence they came.

Jacob was frozen from shock as he leaned over the wall. "I *knew* this would happen somehow!" he shouted at himself. "You imbecile! You take her on these sales campaigns as though you're voyaging to Messina or Palermo!"

He kept screaming at himself while nervously running his fingers through his thick hair. Suddenly, his peripheral vision caught Prince Peter riding back into the castle ahead of the other knights. He ran to the square to try to speak with the prince, but he was stopped by the sentry.

"Hey, merchant! Where do you think you are going?"

"I have certain maps of Rogenshire that will help the prince get the damsels back," Jacob stated with as much unemotional candor as he could possibly muster.

"Oh! Is that so?" mocked the sentry. "Who says we're going to get them?"

"Well, ah ..." Jacob stammered. He was not prepared for such apathy.

"All rescues are the king's matter first! We must hear our king!"

"Well, of course. Yes ..." said Jacob, "that's exactly where I was going, to the court."

"You are not allowed in the court!" yelled the sentry.

"*Let him through!*" came a handsome bass voice from the blond-haired prince as he removed his helmet and dismounted his destrier. "Whoa, Montgomery." Prince Peter patted his horse on the neck and handed the reins and helmet to his squire John Luke, who had just arrived on the scene after watching his master from the gate tower. (John Luke had found the watchman at post there *asleep*. That is why the peasantry had not been warned! Needless to say, he awoke the sentry by dumping a shovel full of horse dung from the stable on him and leaving dung and dummy in the tower!)

"*Bien garde*, Montgomery!" Montgomery whinnied with a slight moan attached, as if to say, "How can I guard well when no one warns us of the enemy coming?" The disillusioned yet obedient, strong fighting horse, along with his master's helmet, was taken to the stable.

"Jacob Santoro, we meet again!" Prince Peter gave Jacob a friendly slap on the shoulder and greeted him as an equal as he took the gauntlet off his right hand and shook Jacob's bare hand. The courtiers just stared. This prince was known for his "innovations" and Christian charities with every class of society, but betimes they thought him really quite amusing in loving everybody.

There were already rumors about him and his affections for the peasant Cassandra. The crowd of gentry beneath him in social rank bowed low and curtsied as he turned from Jacob to them, but when their eyes met his, he knew he was standing alone for the idea of a rescue, if there ever would be one.

"Don't be concerned, Jacob," whispered Prince Peter as he leaned back to the man, "I love being on the side of the disadvantaged; it has always been a wonderful challenge for me."

"Good for you, sire," Jacob replied, yet in his mind he was not at all contented.

"My father will not want to bother with a rescue," whispered the prince to Jacob as they both walked up the castle steps with the same stride.

"But … he has to!" pleaded Jacob. "Doesn't he care about his own people?"

"No, he doesn't care about them at all, I'm afraid," the prince said in a deep and perplexed anger. "The only thing he seems to care about is his wine! Wine is fine if drunk in moderation, but he uses it as a mistress … my dear late mother's competition."

The sentries at the castle doors interrupted the prince's mournful explanation as they crossed their spears in front of the two men. "Your father the king will speak to you alone, Prince Peter," stated one. "We were told to arrest this Jew for treason. There were maps to Rogenshire found in his belongings at the inn this morning. The king believes that he told someone about the commoners' passageway through the forest to our kingdom. He is to stand trial this afternoon for the loss of our peasantry."

"What! That is preposterous! I won't hear of it!" shouted the prince as the guards of the dungeon grabbed Jacob. The prince tried to stop them but was quickly and meanly slapped to the ground by an armored hand. He leaned on his shoulder and fought the oncoming blackout. Thus encircled by the sentries to the castle, he screamed out to Jacob, who had just been given a more severe blow to the head and was being dragged away, "I will find them Jacob! I will try to arrest your trial. This is – "

"Watch your tongue, son!" gloated his father with hands on hips, crown on head, and staunch stance on the top stair. "I will see him alone!" he shouted. The prince just looked up the stone staircase as the sentries retreated from their circle and took their posts; he knew he was in for another rough ride.

Chapter B:

The Iron Man with the Cross on His Gold Spurs

"Sit down, son," the king said in a kind voice when they were finally alone in the royal eating hall. The prince, hurt, hungry, and heartily beaten in every way possible, almost fell into the crimson-cushioned chair girded with ivory from the tusks of gigantic animals that once lived in lands far away. The prince, for one moment, turned his head, gazed at one side of his chair, and mused about an escape to a land so distant. His father looked at the black-and-blue bruise now forming on the side of his son's otherwise handsome visage.

"Look at the book in front of you," said the king in an almost melancholy tone. "The grapes and cheese on the table are waiting to be eaten, son," the king continued. "I want your opinion on this manuscript; you've become quite the erudite knight. I am going to my scribe's quarters, only for a while. When I return, we will talk and then feast on meats and discuss your birthday celebration. In a very short time, you'll be a quarter century old!" The king walked toward the private doors to the royal quarters and was through them before the prince could speak a thank you or a protest.

Exhausted and ravaged by hunger, the young warrior picked grapes and plopped them in his mouth and chewed, in spite of the incredible pain to the upper part of his cheek by his eye. The cheese was brie, from lands across the dividing sea, and the bread he put it on was not stale but fresh, fit for royalty. "Thank you, Lord Jesus, for your body and your blood." He looked at the manuscript and read. It was a copy of one of the works written by a Rogenshire king years ago. The man was dark in heart and his deeds were a twisted delirium of continuous self-applause and grandeur. The book was exceptionally well written, but the philosophy was not based on love and service at all. "I don't know what one would call it," the scholar said to himself, "but the economy of this king gave no thought for the poor or the lower gentry. The tradesman usually has say in his work, at least; however, in this book, he seems to be used as dung for the crops in the fields. The squire, the widow, and the stranger are treated much the same as this ... everything is centered on the king as if he had taken the place of God Himself." Closing the book with a bang, his head aching from injury, the prince placed his hand on the belted side of his right eye and jerked upright; the pain was piercing, "I can no longer deal with this darkness." He shook his head slowly and finished the bread, with every bite taken as a delicate doll would chew. The goblet of water was mixed with wine and it was full. "Of course, dear father would leave me this, generous heart that he is." He chuckled sarcastically and drank until he was done.

"Well, how do you like it?" The king smiled as he returned after a short while, as he had promised. The royal son noticed he even looked happy and was not totally drunk.

"Have you taken up a new hobby, father?" he asked, a little perplexed.

"No son," answered the king, still smiling with contentment. "How do you like it?"

"Oh, yes ... the food was great," said the son, patting his painful bruise.

"No, no, no," answered the king, "I meant the manuscript. It's a true way to conduct a kingdom, is it not?"

"Hmm ... father." Prince Peter knew his battles had probably only just begun as he quickly thanked God for the small sustenance that he had received and allowed the blessed Holy Spirit to work through his thoughts, heart, and voice. "Father, I read this manuscript years ago, and it is very well written."

"Yes! Yes! It is very well written, son. I knew you would see it!"

"Father, if Satan himself, who was probably an exceptionally gifted writer, could write anything in the flesh, this is the very manuscript he would have written."

"What did you say?" The king's voice finished on a high and loud note, signifying that another philosophical argument would ensue. This time, he had incited his own son to state what was in his heart and soul. He was heir to the kingdom, and the king would make sure today and finally in the maturity of this prince's personage whether or not he chose the king's cause.

"Father, sir, you heard what I said. This way of thinking is totally contrary to the Code of Chivalry, which all good Christian knights are mandated to practice. It is against our customs and our way of life."

"To the dungeon with chivalry! To the rack with Christian knighthood! To the depths of hell for any stranger who shared with us these practices and laws in the first place!"

"Father, these practices and way of life came from the sacred books most monks copy. The priests read these every Sunday! They are the moral fabric of anything positive in our culture. Take them away and you'll – "

"I'll take them away! I'm sick of bowing down to *love*! There is no other God here than *myself*! I am God!"

"You are not God, Father! Be careful with your words." The prince's father knew exactly which chord to hit inside this instrument of faithfulness. He wanted to see if there was a change, a would-be compromise ... there was none. The sturdy love of his dead mother and her charity from a forgotten era lingered long in the son's mind, heart, and body, and he boldly proclaimed it without hesitation. "We are created in His image, Father, but we are not Him!"

"Whose image?" screamed the father.

The son had hit the father's chord now; he had suffered consequences before. "A Jew from Nazareth, Father. We are created in God's likeness and the decision to send a Jew to save us all was the High Father's choice – not mine and not yours!" The son's eyes, pierced with pain, looked straight through his father's, so much so that the man rocked back in step.

"That's enough! You are outdated, outflanked, outlawed, and a lost cause to antiquity!" the king continued with a vehemence that had become normal for his person as of late. "I will no longer tolerate the sacred Scripture readings on Sunday in Latin or any other language!"

"But the poor will not hear the gospel!" shouted the prince.

"If you really care about them so much, why don't you join them!" The sentries in the private doorway closed in. The prince had made his final decision, and it was not in his favor.

"Wait! My priest!" shouted Prince Peter with a desperate voice, his palm poised in the air, facing his father.

"No son, *my* priest, and it seems as if he will never be yours!"

"What will you do with him? He always explains the Scripture every Sunday for anyone who will listen." Prince Peter was standing now; he placed his hand on the hilt of his sword. He knew his father had gone completely mad, but he had become a knight. He could never choose darkness and he was determined to fight for the light.

"I'll nail 'old faithful' to the rack! The priest from Rogenshire can visit once a week!" shouted the mad man with a heinous chuckle.

"Oh my God in heaven!" One last phrase of a shocked, innocent boy came from the mouth of the iron man standing upright.

"Go ahead! Call on Him! He won't answer you!" mocked the king threateningly. "I doubt you'll make it to your twenty-fifth year!"

"You would rack the priest who helped to bring me up, taught me languages and the sciences of God? You would mutilate a man of the cross who was my parent?" lamented Prince Peter, summing up evil intent in one wretched moment.

"Enough of your blubbering! You are a philosophically illegitimate stranger! Guards! Take the armor off this one-time son! Throw him into the cell with the Jew. Since he likes the Scriptures so much, then to the people of these Scriptures he shall go!"

Two sentries finished their hustle through the private chambers and six through the front entrance way. The final trap had been set for Prince Peter. Choosing the side of the Father in Heaven, the Prince mourned for Heartland as he whipped out his sword from its sheath with his right hand, and with his left grabbed the dagger from his right thigh.

"*Sentries stand still!*" ordered Prince Peter in a bellowing voice much louder than his father's that seemed to vibrate the stone walls around them all. The sentries stopped suddenly; they knew the master knight and his ambidexterity. His mastery of arms was at its prime and so was his strength. This iron man was no longer the shy, abused boy they once knew, and had not been for some time.

"You have no authority over my guards, you philosophical orphan!" yelled the father, backing up toward the private chamber doors.

Ignoring his father's last mind battle, his eyes strained toward the sentries, looking right through them. "Sentries, listen to reason! You would take for slaughter your prince and follow the foul order of this fiend in my father who would slaughter you next! He doesn't care about you! *I will fight! I will win by God's grace!* The kingdom will not be taken by darkness, and those damsels will be rescued by the powerful arm of glory!"

"It will have to be God's grace and glory only, my lord," said one of the sentries. "Your father is still king."

"You would stand behind wickedness?" Prince Peter's eyes widened with incredulity.

"He hasn't said anything to us, my lord," the same sentry stated with a nervous demeanor. The others looked at each other, not used to thinking on their own. They seemed to the prince to be trying to gather each other's opinions with their thoughts alone.

"My father feeds your families well, but what about the others?" shouted the royal, hoping to place one pinch of charity into their minds to shatter their greed and fears.

"We are fed, prince!" said the spokesman sentry and, without another thought, he lunged forward.

The sentry's right-armed sword was raised to come down hard on the warrior who would stand alone. The swiftness of the iron man's left-handedness thrust the distanced dagger right into the man's unprotected throat. As his sword dropped, so did his body, onto its knees first before the sentry fell dead, flat on his face. Prince Peter pierced open the belly of another sentry flanked to his right as he drove the sword in his right hand deep and hard up through the slit in the man's breast and pelvic armor. Continuing to hold his sword in a dripping red release from the still-standing dead body, the master knight did an iron semi-pirouette to thrust the same sword through another belly flanked to his left. "My father should update his sentries' armor!" laughed the prince, mocking his enemies, thus undoing the stability of their minds before their bodies. He had learned the trick of mental warfare all too well. He quickly picked up the dripping dagger with his left hand from a dead throat still pulsating with the dreams of life and finished the fourth in an upward sweep through the groin.

"There are four down, Heartland!" shouted the winning royal. "Or am I speaking to another kingdom?!"

"You are too good, iron man!" whined another sentry from a small distance. "Why do you go against your father?" The sentry was stalling for time but was truly puzzled; he seemed like another ox having to make a choice between turning right or left without the help of a yoke.

"There are still four of us, iron man!" shouted another.

"Four mere men are no match for a knight with the cross on his gold spurs!" shouted the prince back to them.

They did not listen, and he did not answer as to why. This was a fight to the death. His father, the king, was frozen at the chamber doors; he said nothing.

Prince Peter turned and ran the other way as if to retreat, and the four men followed. He ran up the six gold-plated stone stairs that lead to the throne, behind which was an inner chamber to which presumably only the king had a key. Puzzled and trained to never go beyond this invisible line, the men stopped at the foot of the very wide but longitudinally small staircase. A chandelier of iron and wood hung overhead, forged and carved by Prince Peter himself as he learned some points of each trade in his kingdom throughout his teen years. He also made wheels of wood atop the ceiling that rolled on iron rims so the same chandelier above the throne could glide to the table at the great hall's center, which now was more than a few steps behind the men.

Holding one sword and grabbing the iron shepherd's crook leaning up against the high wall used to pull the chandelier to the table, Prince Peter bounded off the highest stair and hung on with an iron grip, crimping his body like a snail to make the works move that much faster to the table. He managed to slice off one man's head before reaching it. Getting back to a standing position while turning, the knight saw the three men left still running toward him and the table that would separate them, one on each end and a dumb one at the head. Just what the iron man ordered – three men caught at table, and he had all the height he needed. Taking full advantage of his superior position on the old durable oak table inlaid with mahogany, he finished his job in a second or two.

Chapter 4:

A Martyr's Final Prophecy

"Well done, iron man!" shouted the cowardly father as he ran through the private doors and slammed them shut. Prince Peter heard the wooden plank fall on the iron bolts on the other side, blocking his entrance. "Little time is left to me here," Prince Peter whispered to himself as he jumped off the table via a plush crimson-cushioned chair with a bold ivory frame and ran out the front door.

"Where is the priest?" he shouted to a gentlewoman standing just outside in a small crowd that had gathered to hear the outcome. The prince grabbed her shoulders gently but firmly and shook her just a little in his desperation.

Her answer was expedient, "He is at the altar preparing the Host himself, my lord."

"Thank you," said the desperate seeker, letting her go and running off to the sole servant who had really raised him. Flinging open the heavy wooden doors overlaid with bronze depicting the death of the Lord Jesus on the left and His resurrection on the right, the prince was ensconced immediately by bright sunlight flooding through the opening and illuminating the center aisle up to the altar where the priest was at work. The beautiful stained glass images of the saints on the side of the chapel echoed their sunlight in various waves of color, praising the glory of the sudden secret meeting about to take place.

"You must escape, Brother Barnabas!" Prince Peter shouted before he was hardly at the rear of the aisle.

"Escape?" Brother Barnabas stopped his work and looked up. He saw the prince's blond hair flailing in time with his stride, and the blackness of the right side of his face was pronounced by the light. "Oh, Peter! What have you done now? We did not defeat the enemy in combat?" said the monk-priest.

"Not yet," said Prince Peter, coming up to the altar. He grabbed the monk by the shoulders and brought them both down to a sitting position on the Master's staircase before His table and presence.

"I have just slain the king's sentries," confessed the warrior to his adopted parent, who looked at this iron man always as his child.

"You cannot win this battle with your chain mail or breastplate, my son," explained the teacher of Jesus in a moroseness becoming only to aliens of this world and lovers of God.

"I had no choice; it was either my armor and my life or theirs," explained the prince emphatically. "Besides, we have a great loss. Cassandra is taken and so is Tirzah. Her father Jacob is now in the dungeon and they are coming to get you!"

"My God!" said the monk-priest, aghast. "They took Jacob? He is innocent."

"I know he is innocent, Brother Barnabas. He told me himself that he had maps this morning, and in the past he always used them only for his trade, nothing more."

"I have them," confessed the priest.

"What!" exclaimed the prince with a bit of glee.

"I heard you and that father of yours come into the great hall this morning, and was about to leave – "

"How did you know we were there?" the prince interrupted.

"Your father thinks he is the only one with the inner chamber key, but I had our loyal blacksmith make a copy a long time ago, after this king favored the scribe who is of Rogenshire stock."

"Brother Barnabas, you mean Rogenshire *thought*. I'm half Rogenshire stock, but I hate the way they think. It's the heart that counts. What you taught me is true."

They both heard the whinnying of horses approaching with the hangman's cart behind them, and a lustful, growing crowd at the stern of an evil plan.

"There is no time, son," said the teacher. "Here are the maps." He produced them from under his cloak; they both stood up.

"I always wondered what kind of 'armor' you monks have, producing shelves of manuscript from your bodies at will!" the prince mumbled as he hastily shoved the handmade cartography below his gambeson wool and chain mail with partial breastplate attached in back and front.

"Remember, son," said the parent sternly, girding his child's leather belt tighter, "we are living epistles or maps to heaven. The way we act in leadership is often how people see God Himself. They may have no other map to go by. No other tool with which to see. I will be taken."

"No! Don't allow yourself this martyrdom, my parent!" The prince started to weep uncontrollably, holding the lover of Jesus in his arms. "You are the only solid, stable thing I have left! You can't do this to me! Who will be my teacher, my guide, my brother, the one who encourages me to live righteously?"

"The blessed Holy Spirit," was the monk's response and, pushing himself away from his child, the look of silence came upon him. "If need be, I will go before Jacob. He has family. This will give you time to rescue the innocent and bleed the guilty if necessary. Although, if the Good Lord wishes, I would request that He give the guilty time to repent of their sins – "

"*There they are!*" came the shout of the king through the two open doors. "*Capture the traitors!*"

"Flee this time, son. This is no time to fight!" Brother Barnabas turned to face the onslaught of angered dungeon guards and castle sentries seeking revenge for the blood of their brethren.

"Revenge is of the Lord!" shouted the brother of God as he walked down the aisle, armed only with the love of the Almighty, and putting himself in-between truth and disaster.

"Then we shall have it!" shouted the king as his armed men encrusted themselves around the sacrifice and chained his hands and feet. As he was pelted with full gauntlets, the prince, unable to repress his weeping, fled through the monk's chambers, out through the narrow back door, and onto the path that lead to the stables. The sentries watched his retreat but were too shaken by his latest successes to follow him.

"Don't follow the one-time royal!" ordered the king, noticing his sentries' hesitation. "He will be killed or caught by Rogenshire. If they ask for a ransom, I will demand a hanging!" All the sentries and guards laughed but were interrupted by a soft, feeble, dying voice.

"You know they won't ask for a ransom, traitor king," whispered the faithful monk in fatal agony, "but your days are numbered. Our knight will return and take the kingdom from you. Righteousness will be restored." Those were the final words of the prophet-priest; the painful effort to speak the truth used up the last morsel of strength he had left after the iron pelting. A white dove from the chapel rafters alit to the skies above as the martyr of Jesus gave up the ghost.

Chapter 5:

Stratagem to Answer the Call of Freedom

John Luke had finished grooming Montgomery, and the champion horse's white hide had just been covered with the royal blue-and-gold caparison. His white mane with silver-blonde streaks had been lavishly and lovingly combed and left hanging long over his stout and muscular neck. The knight and his steed were a perfect pair when the high-backed saddle was filled.

"John Luke, listen to me," said the prince as he looked down sternly from the saddle. His eyes were still draining their tears. "I cannot stop crying, for Heartland has been sorely bruised this day."

"What has happened, master?" asked the innocent youth.

"My father is a wretch," admitted the knight finally with no more denial in his soul.

"We all knew and feared this, dear Prince Peter," said the youth, bowing his head.

"Fear nothing except God," warned the prince. "It is much too late for anything else. Heartland peasants have been slaughtered or taken, a dear friend's daughter has been kidnapped with them, and he is held in the dungeon like a skinned animal before the cutting. I have no more time to even think, never mind rescue. Our parent monk may have become a martyr by now."

"Oh no, no sir!" exclaimed John Luke and started to weep himself at the news of the monk who was parent and teacher to all squires there, as was his duty from God and the joy of his heart.

"Cassandra is all that matters to me the most." Prince Peter sighed out loud. "I must get to her ... if those poor thieves have touched her, I will kill every single one of them with my bare hands." The knight wrenched out the anger from his gut, "I am human and betimes am in need of more humility, John Luke. Take from me lessons of goodness and forget what else I have said that is evil. Jesus the Christ is the perfect One. I feel like a wretched dog at the moment for I think we have been betrayed all round."

"No master. You have not many faithful knights, but their squires are different," the crying squire said as some help from his heart sounded out to his knight and prince.

"How many can you truly trust, John Luke, who may halfway wield the sword?" questioned the knight.

"Only two and the old blacksmith, Paul," answered John Luke with a wink of hope.

"Get to these two youths" directed Prince Peter, "and tell them to wait for you by the tree rooted near the small back dungeon door in the castle wall. Have them hide in the tree if necessary, for they risk their lives siding with you, John Luke. You are my squire, and my father will seek to take you to dictate a following or kill you as well. He doesn't know that you side with Jesus. Run to Paul's house – not his forge, but his home in the back. Do not talk to his apprentice; I do not trust the boy."

"Neither do I," agreed John Luke.

"Very well, then. Obtain an iron object with which to cut through chains. You must free Jacob; there will be no fair trial today. His time to live is decreasing as we speak. The chapel should be closed by now, the damage done ... find the copy of the inner chamber key – "

"I know where it is in Brother Barnabas' private chambers! He had me sneak into the room a few fortnights ago when he was meeting with your father at chapel. I was to steal back some sane documents of ours that the king was going to take to the Rogenshire scribe to 'rewrite.' I replaced them with some nonsense our monk made just for his competition. I just did as I was told."

"How come you never told me?" asked the prince.

"Brother Barnabas said you were praying and fasting for your father to seek repentance. He said this would interrupt your thoughts."

"God love our merciful and practical monk!" chuckled the knight as the tears dried on his face.

"He said you were also praying for our enemies," confessed the youth.

"And so I was," stated the knight. "Jesus said that one's enemies would be members of one's own house, and strangers would become best friends. Our prophet Savior was wise. Some situations never change."

"So I should enter the inner chamber with the key, master?" asked the squire.

"Yes, and go alone. Tell your friends nothing but that they may be helping you to drag Jacob to the safety of the peasants' huts using the small door in the wall."

"Yes, master. That door is in the castle wall. But the moat is full!"

"About ten years ago, the old hemp maker, Cassandra's father, and I fashioned a steadfast rope bridge."

"I've heard of the story, sire. The two iron horse polls still stand erect on the opposite wall," said John Luke. "The sentries, I have heard, mock them from time to time and point to the small door."

"Yes, it is good that fools never venture through wise cracks in a wall, John Luke," stated Prince Peter. "I check on that rope with its lasso every three full moons; it is still in fine condition. How are you with the lasso?"

"I am afraid not that good, but one of the squires for whom I spoke could pull a flying hawk from the sky if he really wanted to do so," said the squire confidently.

"Good. After you rescue Jacob, get inside that door in the wall of the castle. You'll have to open the opposing door, and outside, directly across the moat, you'll see the iron polls with the huts in the far background. Focus each lasso to the iron polls. As you pull on the two ropes, the rope bridge will unfold from its place right in the middle of you with the other boy pulling the other rope. Have the third squire secure the rope bridge by putting the huge iron hooks through the two iron horizontal pillars bolted securely into the stone wall just outside the door. Do all this labor when the door facing the sentries' dungeon entrance is fully shut. Also close the door near the two hooks before you cross the bridge with Jacob. I pray the good Lord causes some sort of amusement for the tower lookout. He is sure to see the bridge. May the angels of God or even the devils themselves deter him from his watch."

"Master! Watch your words," warned John Luke.

"I'm watching them just as I pray the lookout isn't watching at all!" sulked the master on his horse.

"This will be a miracle performed, master," admitted the brave squire, looking up to his lord. "But how is Jacob to be rescued from the dungeon?"

"Take your sword, son. You are fairly good with it. I killed eight sentries today, so there are fewer to be concerned about. Do you remember the unicorn tapestry hanging on the wall inside the inner chamber?"

"The huge one with the virgin, the unicorn, and the secret garden?" asked the squire.

"Yes," said the knight. "Behind that is another small door that uses the same key. It unlocks into a secret staircase that leads to a private library next to the dungeon. Father used it to listen in on guards' conversations to see if any treachery toward his person was afoot. Mother once said that her father, the late king here, used to actually read in it. There were scrolls on shelves at one time where only torture implements now reside. The late king used to meet with guards and speak with the very few prisoners there. There were no torture devices even in the dungeon before my father."

"Really?" stated the boy in surprise.

"I guess this is true, John Luke ... I would believe my angel mother. There are keys to every cell and human cage hanging on iron hooks on the wall just above the oak desk. Those will help you. You must be brave, my young friend. You are Jacob's hope."

"Actually, I give myself to the Lord so He may move me and be Jacob's hope for me," said the squire with the humility that befits a good knight.

"Well said, John Luke," encouraged Prince Peter. "You are right. I cannot lead you from here. The Holy Spirit will be your guide and protector. I must ride swiftly. Pray He is my protector as well." The prince reached his gauntlet and long arm down and grabbed John Luke in a semi-embrace as Montgomery bent his knees just a little and whinnied some hope and praise to his Creator for the journeys they were all about to undertake.

Prince Peter let go of his squire, and they both secretly moved to the back door of the well-established stable. John Luke quickly used the pulley to let the stable drawbridge down so the prince and Montgomery could alight themselves from what had become a prison. The guards at the back towers were not even there, as they were a part of the "pelting celebration" of heaven's newest martyr. John Luke closed the drawbridge door almost as swiftly as he had opened it. Prince Peter and Montgomery flew onto the back path of the forest; their hope was Jacob's survival and the accuracy of his maps. The prince's only longing desire was to regain the women back, especially his beloved Cassandra, and regain Heartland as a king loyal to *love.*

The saints and angels witnessed the capture of a fellow soul in the chambers of holiness as the chapel doors were firmly shut by intruders and the only light came from the sky through the stained glass windows on the side of the little church. As the sun shone, a faint glow alighted by the Host left on the altar table (or was it the strange glass of a monocular?) reflected one steady and faithful deep violet-red ray. One strand of hope, one ray of glory, one God of Israel, and only a few faithful souls left to answer the call of truth.

Chapter 6:

The Secret Abode of a Masquerading Royal

The Rogenshire ride through the forest happened roughly but without incident as the dark knights slowed down but kept a steady pace. Their cheap "joy of the joust" was over and they knew full well a rescue party would never be sent. By midmorning they arrived at the very familiar old inn. Some of them let loose their prey while others held on to them with a bear's grip, dragging their captured waifs off the steeds to bruise them even more.

"Hah! So my crystals were right ... and you have come," said the proprietor, an old goat of a lady, to the captors as she walked out her front door, pail in hand. The well was twenty paces to the left of the inn's front entrance and at the bottom of the large knoll the house rested on. She noticed Tirzah through the corner of her eye but wisely continued to invite the wicked knights to dine. "Knowing you would arrive, I have prepared wild turkeys and some luscious roast goose that traveled here too early and got caught in my nets!" She winked at Tirzah, one of those let loose, who winked back. Cassandra said nothing, and neither did the others, as iron grips finally let them all loose with the promise of food.

Laughing uproariously as only hags can, she set the tone and flavor of their feast, and the hideous knights followed suit in laughter and bombarded her humble abode. Seeing the food most definitely already there on a huge wooden table, they commenced their squandering of every morsel and expected prompt service.

"Wench, I need more water!" yelled one of them to a serf girl.

The captives commenced their service at table as the hag took Tirzah aside. "It's going to be a little harder escape this time because there are more of you, my dear. Same old way though … always works!"

"You mean your kitchen?" muttered Tirzah.

"Of course my kitchen, you silly thing," she stated. "I heard Rogenshire is preparing a mock banquet for these poor peasant wenches. The evil young prince there says he will pretend to marry them all but make none of them his queen!"

Tirzah was too stunned to respond.

"I don't think there will be a rescue attempt, dearie," the wise old woman added. "I heard through the grapevines in the forest that this kidnapping was a trade-off between Peter's father and my evil brother. I would believe it; he tried to kill me, his older sister, years ago – you know this. Keep it a secret still, Tirzah."

"Father and I always have, your majesty," said Tirzah. "To everyone, you are just 'the old innkeeper.'"

"How is Jacob?" asked the hidden majesty who was once Princess Grace, heir to a throne.

"Wench!" yelled Tirzah's captor to her. "I need more turkey! Hurry up!"

Tirzah ran to the only adjacent room and found some of the others searching for food, but finding nothing other then a few small windows, a straw bed, a few rags of clothing on hooks, a small and rickety old table, a tiny wooden fireplace, a few herbs, and an empty tea mug, they looked a little panicked and bewildered. "The food is below us," said Tirzah from her memory, smiling ever so slightly.

"She is right, my darlings," said the wise one, rushing in. She shouted behind her to the fools of wickedness in her eating room, "They'll be right out with more turkey! Do you want more gravy with that?"

"Of course, you old hag!" bellowed more than one of them.

Tirzah had opened a hatch door underneath a worn-out Persian rug and commenced her descent down the small wrought iron circular staircase as she looked up at the hag and said, "We'll have to get you a new rug – on the house." The undercover princess smiled a very warm, nearly toothless smile.

"Your father always pulled through for me, as I tried to do for him," she whispered. "Hurry, my pretties, fill the handcrafted stairs."

The young peasants were a bit astonished but they obeyed readily. Tirzah had them form a line and passed the turkey and the gravy up one to another. The last two brave maidens went out with the innkeeper to put all the food on the table. A third went out to the well to draw water and returned to fill all their goblets.

"Place the extra water on the table, little wench," stated the innkeeper firmly to the serf girl. "Follow me into the kitchen quickly – they will want more service, right gentlemen?"

Nothing but laughter smoldered in turkey meat and fat was their response. Her wine had long since been found by one of the knights and the barrel was a quick friend to all.

They started targeting the almost empty wine barrel with silver coins, as was their normal custom when they passed through the forest and stopped to eat at the inn. The soon-to-be ex-innkeeper stuffed a sackcloth with her clothes and the tea mug in the adjacent room, ready to protect herself, as was her normal custom with inconsiderate customers such as these. She then grabbed her rabbit cloak from the old straw bed and forced all the maidens down her staircase.

"I'm not coming back here for a while," she whispered to Tirzah, closing the trap door above them quietly. She then elbowed her way to the bottom of the line and the foot of the stairs. "If they don't burn my place down, I'll be lucky; nonetheless, luck may not be with me. Everyone knows I always hated the wickedness of that self-proclaimed tyrant of Rogenshire. An innkeeper has much say in the forest …" She muttered to herself as she made her way to a gigantic brick fireplace and extinguished the fire as quickly as possible, then took all the pots and utensils out of it and put them on the huge oak table, which took up most of the room. Tirzah helped her as the others just watched in confusion. Cassandra noticed the stone-and-mud walls and the small windows right near the top of the wooden ceiling covered with woven reeds so as not to be completely noticed. Thick books on worn-out shelves covered one wall entirely while well-used oriental rugs covered the other walls for warmth and culture.

"Rip me those rugs off the wall and be quick!" whispered Princess Grace to Cassandra. Cassandra, in a fright, obeyed and, grabbing the rugs, the woman hurled one down on the cinders and the other she threw inside the fireplace wall. Then with a small shout she said, "Every maid in the fireplace quickly! Shove yourselves together now! Hurry, they'll be wanting service at any moment!"

The young women were in too much of a shock not to comply with her, and noticing Tirzah working right along with her, they all wedged themselves into the fireplace, feeling the heat from the cinders come up through the rugs to the soles of their feet. Tirzah then pulled one of two latches and the whole fireplace started to turn.

"What is happening?" said Cassandra as hope sprang up in her belly at the thought of a successful escape.

The maids seemed attached to each other; they were cloistered together as the whole fireplace made a one-hundred-eighty-degree turn and stopped as suddenly as it had started without one squeak.

Tirzah seemed to know right where the torch was cradled in a wooden cage nailed to the quarry stone wall, and as she lit it, a strong, continuous, unflickering flame showed another smaller adjacent secret chamber. The captured, now almost free, looked in amazement at one another and at a small door directly at the other end.

"What is that wooden pull ring hanging from the middle of the ceiling for?" asked one of the maids.

"Oh," said the princess, "that's another way out, but I haven't used it in so long I've forgotten how it works. The top of this place, where those reprobates are now, has been burned down twice already. This inn is my third building on the same foundation. I think this was an exit for the second inn. Right now, we are going straight ahead."

"Why was it burned down twice?" asked another maid.

"Sometimes these knights don't follow the chivalry code that their Christian God has supposedly put into their hearts, but they deem themselves gods of their own fates."

"And?" the young maid still questioned.

"And ... well ... what does it matter? They drink too much and get stupid or they get angry. Fights start and fires begin. It is a miracle that my books have never burned ..." She walked toward the door, dragging her sack and one of the rugs behind her when there was a thud somewhere above them and then a moment of silence.

"They know we are gone!" said one maid out loud.

"Shh! Silence. They may or may not hear us. The wooden floor is above a thick layer of stone and mud. Just wait," said the princess innkeeper.

They waited and shortly afterward heard the sounds of clashing, banging, breaking, and the crackling of kindled fire.

"Oh, good night! I'm getting too old for this!" exclaimed the princess as she banged her sack against the stone wall. "They must have used my small fireplace. I built that one myself. Now we have to wait here because the tunnel I also built, which I wanted to take, may not be sturdy with all this destruction. I also do not know which way these menacing men will go. We could leave into the forest and they could find us right out in the open."

"Why are we safe here?" a panic-stricken maid asked.

"Because the same person who built the iron staircase, the fireplace, and invented the works that move it is the same man who made the foundation to the inn of which this secret room is a part." Princess Grace comforted herself with this knowledge and sat down on her rabbit cloak as she leaned up against one of the foundation walls. The others followed suit as they heard the muffled destruction above them.

The dark knights above the secret chamber noticed their waifs were not waiting on them at all, and after they received no response to their calls, they were totally vexed. Looking into the adjacent room, they found only a small wooden fireplace, an old straw bed, a rickety old table, and an overused Persian rug on the floor. Thinking their little foxes had escaped through the small back door opposite the straw bed, they lit the house on fire to embitter their traitor hostess, as they thought she was, and mounted their steeds, leaving only small parts of their armor behind them. They looked forward to a merry hunt through the forest, not noticing the ominous clouds of rain beginning to gather.

While the house above them burned to its foundation for the third time, there were many questions to answer.

"What are all your names?" asked the traitor to the darkness.

"You first!" said Cassandra, who was beginning to realize that this innkeeper was more than an innkeeper.

"Me ... hah! I've lived too long. To be safe, I am just a middle-aged hag with crystals, but as of late I have thought of returning to my first love. I have not prayed to Him for a long time."

Princess Grace's eyes grew clearer and began to sparkle as if a shadow of dullness was released, an old life burned to dust, and a new one just beginning. "Saving all of you today brought the selfless love back into my heart, something that hasn't been there for years."

"But you have saved father and me in times past," said Tirzah.

"And he saved me, my love," said Princess Grace. "Your father was my secret love, the builder and designer of this foundation and all the dwellings that were atop it – with the help of the forest folk. The mud and stone above you and the fireplace with its movable works are all your father's design and the work of his hands many, many years ago, before you voyaged with him."

"Why did he do all this?" asked a suddenly shocked Tirzah, still seated and holding the torch.

"I saved his life when I was a mother with a child – a son," Princess Grace admitted, coming out of her secret shell. She looked around her and saw nothing but nine pairs of eyes sparkling in the torch's twilight; she had a captive audience and time to tell the tale.

Chapter 7:

The Mason's Romance Made Known and the Dragon's Torch

"At one time, I did not look like this," mused the princess out loud, her grey eyes sparkling with a fire not at all like the destructive flames above her. "I looked more like one of you in all your beauty." She pointed a knobby finger at her audience. "I was once Princess Grace of what is now Rogenshire."

All the young maids gasped so loudly and with the same momentum that it sounded as though a short rush of wind had swept through a secret chamber. "Jacob Santoro, although still handsome I hear, was striking in his youth, and a little naïve in those days." She chuckled. "As a princess, I had right to tell him with which kingdoms he could best do business because of their honesty and integrity. Rogenshire, as you know, was not one of them."

The maids tittered at that comment as the princess continued, "We would meet out here in the forest, when he came up to sell to Heartland. After a time I was often invited there by Prince Peter's grandfather, who was still king then. May he rest in peace." Her face bent down toward the dirt as she mourned holy memories. "I tell you, when a righteous man goes to glory it suits heaven better, but the loss on earth can be too much to bear."

"Well, why did you become … a forest dweller?" asked a maid.

"Ha! Bad politics my friend! You see, Prince Peter's grandfather was a good man, but my father was not. When my father, then king, found out about my endearments toward Jacob, he forbade me to meet with him again. Nonetheless, in spite of this, I would sneak out of my kingdom to see Jacob in this very forest. The good king of Heartland could do nothing about our illicit rendezvous when we were caught. I escaped the tower afterward by way of long hemp rope and the cliff wall that has a stairway for soldiers dug into it. I freed Jacob from the dungeon with the help of Providence and my sword, and we lived with the forest folk until my new identity was well installed, and his profession remained intact with the other kingdoms. My title was revoked when I was in the tower. All of Rogenshire believes me to be dead. It is so strange that all these years I have been a communicator of sorts, and living so close to the castle I once called home but have never been able to go back." Princess Grace said her last sentence whimsically, with no regret on her face. "The good king died, I believe, shortly after Peter was born. Prince Peter thinks I am dead as well. Only your father, Tirzah, has known the truth."

"So you two came out here, where you had secretly met," said one of the maids. "But who taught you how to use the sword?"

"They were going to rack and then severe him," stated the princess with a moan. Her eyes kept staring ahead into a world the others could not see. "The least I could do was save him since I was the reason for his peril." She suddenly looked at her audience with a blink. "I knew the castle all too well and was able to make a fine escape for him."

"How?" asked her audience in unison.

"Fortunately, there was a monk in our kingdom much like the one now in Heartland – Brother Barnabas, I believe is his name?"

"Yes!" chimed her audience. They all knew and loved him.

"This monk, Brother George, was a bold knight before he took the cloth. He taught me the skill of the sword. He also told me wonderful stories of Faithland before it turned into Rogenshire." She sighed. "I used the sword in defense of Jacob in the dungeon. I obtained the keys by way of my rank, opened the door, and went to slaughter."

"How many guards did you kill?" asked Cassandra, as the rest were in too much shock to speak.

"Seven in all," she stated without emotion. "I did not want to kill them, but it seems they wanted to torture an innocent man. The only thing he was guilty of was being a foreigner and falling in love with a princess."

"But you said you had a son?" asked one.

"Yes, he was Jacob's."

At that, Tirzah let out a small whimper, hardly noticed as everyone else sat in a still silence. The princess smiled.

"It was wrong that we were not wed; nonetheless, good came out of it. Unfortunately, our son died a crib death, and a big part of me died with him the morning I found him not breathing. I don't know why to this day he had to leave me, and from that morning until now I stopped praying to my first love."

The princess took Tirzah's hand and, placing Tirzah's head on her bosom, she comforted the young lady. "Jacob and I never had quite the same relationship after the death of Benjamin, but he and I did have you and he always remained faithful to visit me, and of course, to take refuge when he had to – especially later on when you traveled with him. When you were an infant, he took you to Venice. We both knew life was too hard here, and I would age considerably faster than he because of it. We both thought it best not to tell you anything. I hope he understands when he finds out that you know."

"I should have known from the beginning," stated Tirzah with vexed betrayal. She loosened herself from the princess and for a long while there was complete silence. Only enlightened knowledge danced in the fire of the torch that Cassandra was now holding. Tirzah sat with arms crossed and tears draining slowly from her very hot face. The princess lifted her knotty hand to feel the wrinkles on her face and jowl. Saddened, she dropped her hand and withering arm into her lap and just sat gazing at the brilliant, young eyes that were in shock and surprise before her.

The forever inquisitive Cassandra, still holding the torch, finally broke the tense silence with a question to Tirzah, hoping to change her mood. "How did you light this so fast?"

"Yes, and why did we not hear the fireplace move when we were moving in it?" said yet another maid, coming back to the reality of the present; the flames of fire must have still been whirling in a hellish dance above them.

"To answer the question of the light," said Tirzah, wiping the tears from her face, "it is part of the dragon mystery – look at the torch." All eyes peered closely and saw that the torch was a hollowed-out bone with something that looked like wax inside and a weird looking wick.

"This," said Tirzah, "is part of the inside of a dragon joint." Cassandra shrieked and almost let go of the bone. "Its humor burns for a long time and doesn't smell that much. What smells is the fiery liquid that coats the dragon's mouth and helps the fire come out of it. This weird wick is a piece of the dragon's upper palate in its mouth or the hard lining on the inside that the princess pushed in there. It is almost like tree bark the way it feels. It will continue to burn with the humor. I lit it by rubbing it quickly – just once on the wall."

"The belly substance has long since dried up on the stone there," said Princess Grace. "That is why there is no smell now, but even dry it lights quickly. As long as there is air, it will light well."

"Who killed the dragon?" asked Cassandra.

"I did," said Princess Grace, "only by God's glory and power. How we forget our divine friend when we think something too precious has been taken from us. He saved my life many times. I ought to be grateful and not doubt Him."

"But you used your sword to slay the dragon, did you not?" asked Tirzah.

"Of course, my dear. But what sword is ever any good without the anointing of the Holy One when in a one-to-one encounter with a flying dragon? There is still one left, you know."

"There is?" said the audience with amazement.

"Yes, the female dragon is still alive. If there were any fertilized eggs, she could be harboring young. It takes a long time for a flying dragon to grow – but then they can live long, too."

"How long?" asked one of the maids.

"They can live way over one hundred years, just like the old sea turtles Jacob used to talk about! If a long life is rewarded to them, they may live to be two and sometimes three hundred years old!"

"Why did you kill the dragon?" asked Cassandra.

"Well, that was the first house that was burned down. I guess there was some sort of shortcut or lair these dragons had made near this part of the forest which is closer to the Rogenshire fields, and they felt that my inn was in their way. The second burning occurred because of the bickering and drunkenness of men, as I said before. We always put down dragons, but maybe they might have been acting out of self-preservation and not just the drunken, lunatic idiocy that humans have a problem with sometimes," stated Princess Grace, taking the torch. Her voice had come back to a modular, authoritarian consistency from the past, but her eyes remained static, still staring into a world no one could see.

She looked up with the others and heard the pounding of heavy rain over the top of their heads with peals of thunder and lightning. "The air will not grow stale for a while. We'll stay here as the tunnel is not built with stone; it may get wet because of the rain. We may decide to go out through the chimney. I don't yet know."

"What about the men?" asked a maid.

"Knowing what kind of stupid fools they are," said the princess, "I assume they are hunting for us in the deep woods; they know I am good friends with the forest folk. I feel badly about not being able to warn them, but their men are now armed – every one of them is, actually. So they can defend themselves," answered the princess.

"Who taught them how to defend themselves?" asked Tirzah with a smile. She already knew the answer and had gotten over her shock just a little. It helped to be proud of someone, even when she was not perfect.

"Who do you think?" stated the princess with a wrinkled grin from one ear to another. "We will stay here. It has been raining, and they might stop roaming through the woods to find another fate for themselves. It is most likely they will find the underground lake and hide there until the downpour is over; returning to the Rogenshire king without their prey would be disastrous for them. They may also return near here, so timing our escape is especially important."

"Somebody answer the fireplace question!" said an extremely curious young maid who hadn't yet spoken.

"Oh, yes," laughed the princess, "that was Jacob's pumice and vinegar idea with a pinch of very fine sand from the underground lake. It works really well, doesn't it?"

"Yes!" said Cassandra. "Where is the underground lake?"

"That is near the Rogenshire Castle. As a matter of fact, the river runs right to the lake. The stone of the original castle was mined from a grotto that connects to the lake. It is like an underground beach now. I have heard through the forest grapevines that additions to the castle are now taking place. I hope they don't take too much stone away from certain places."

"Why?" asked Cassandra.

"Because it is likely the castle could cave in or there would be a weakness in the building on a certain side," answered the princess.

The captive audience sat there and began to chuckle together for the first time since their kidnapping. They had made it through the first round, and with an old, royal, wise, and sympathetic lady, they just might make it back to Heartland after all.

Chapter 8

The Children Chide

Meanwhile, back at Heartland, John Luke skirted quickly through the stables to the pathway that led to the monk's chambers. Finding the key inside the monk's Bible at John 3:16, he hurried outside the chamber area into the sanctuary to hustle himself out the side door under one of the stained glass windows when his eye caught the reflection of the monocular. Knowing to whom it belonged, he grabbed it from the Host table and winged himself across the courtyard as fast as he could to the side alleys of the walled village, praying he would not be discovered. The two young squires whom he trusted often kept each other's company on and off work and were together near the bakery when John Luke noticed them.

"Mark and Gregory," said John Luke in plain voice as he came right up next to them, took a coin from his pouch, and traded it for a patisserie as if the news he was about to give was quite normal.

Mark grabbed John Luke by the arm and he and Gregory ran into the side alley next to the bakery and sat behind an ox cart filled with hay. "It is dangerous for you here!" said Mark to John Luke. "They are already looking for you! What is this … Jacob's monocular!" Mark poked the projection coming from John Luke's chest and pulled. While John Luke swallowed his sugary tart, the instrument came into view. John Luke grabbed it back with sticky fingers and looked defiantly at his friend.

"We overheard the king had this and his maps!" said Mark, trying to explain.

"He is already on the rack, John Luke," said Gregory. "They killed our priest, Barnabas, and they might do the same to you unless you recant."

"Recant what?" asked John Luke with somewhat of a mischievous attitude.

"Recant your apprenticeship to your master so you can be given to another. It will spare your life, friend!" answered Gregory with a warm warning for his fellow squire.

"Not with this thing it won't!" said Mark. "Jacob's monocular is supposed to be with the king!"

"Our beloved monk took it from him," answered John Luke. Both youths gasped, their eyes inquisitive.

The young hero continued, "He made a copy of the inner chamber key when the king started to favor the scribe from Rogenshire. He redeemed the instrument from the king this morning, along with everything the king had stolen from Jacob to accuse him falsely."

The two youths looked at each other, knowing they would put themselves in harm's way just siding with their friend or being present with him.

"Listen, I will enter the castle with this key and get Jacob myself, God willing. I just need you two to stay in the tree by the castle wall door and the exit the guards use for the dungeon; they will not see you in the leaved tree. Wait for me there. The door should be unlocked. No one to their knowledge ever uses it – but this key probably works for that door too."

"All we have to do is wait in a tree?" asked Mark, a little perturbed yet relieved.

"Yes, you'll be helping me with the rope bridge once I get Jacob out of the dungeon," explained John Luke.

The youths laughed quietly but heartily at the last statement; the shunted laughter came straight from their bellies as they muted their guffaws with their hands to their mouths. "You mean that mythical invention of the prince? The one that we can't really see but for the two posts at the other side of the moat and there is an invisible bridge that somehow fits inside the wall?" mocked Mark, holding his sides because he was desperately trying to shut up the deep waves of laughter that would just not stop.

"Stop mocking and joking!" John Luke whined the order with more than a bit of trepidation and tears. "It is real and it works with lassos!"

"Oh, I can do that well," said Mark, "but it is usually used when hunting game!"

"Or something that is really moving!" said Gregory, still laughing.

"Oh, Lord, please help me," prayed the young saint. "We need their help if just at the end. Use them, although they taunt you, to wake them up and increase their faith."

"We are not taunting the Lord!" stated Gregory as he immediately stopped laughing. "How can you accuse us of that? We are merely mocking something that doesn't even exist and a problem that just can't be solved." Gregory was so matter-of-fact in speech that even Mark came to his serious senses and listened once again.

"The book of Hebrews says that 'Faith is the substance of things hoped for and the evidence of things unseen,'" John Luke continued. "Since it is a Hebrew we will be saving, I thought that Scripture more than appropriate. Remember, nothing is impossible with God. Do I have an agreement for you two to at least stay in the tree throughout the afternoon lunch? Hopefully, you won't be up there that long."

"Then we can go if poor Jacob doesn't just walk out the door in front of all the guards!" Mark tittered again.

"Yes, quite. Then you can go," said John Luke sadly, wondering to where all the faith in Heartland had escaped.

Chapter 9:

John Luke's Victory, the Hermit's Appearance, and Jacob's Rescue

While Mark and Gregory were going about their merry way just being boys, skipping around the courtyard to the back of the castle and up into the tree, and making light conversation about "this great new hiding place" in front of the two guards who utterly ignored them, John Luke was skillfully manipulating his way through the gentry gathered at the court entrance all the way up to the doors. They were gathered for a fanciful yet quick luncheon of meats in celebration of the king's announcement of the future successor to the throne and memorial for his late son who was just recently eaten by the Rogenshire dragon.

"Who will it be?" said one lovely lady to another as John Luke meandered among the women, sneaked in past the two newly-appointed sentries, and glided along the outer walls of the grand dining hall. He moved as a shadow under the side nave and its column to hide behind the life-size statue of Prince Peter of Heartland in the left front of the gigantic room, the king's statue being on the other side. Looking to view the private chamber door still closed almost in front of him, and waiting for the sentries to be slightly more distracted by the womenfolk now entering the hall and being seated by youths, John Luke abided moments of time. Food started coming in via young men through side doors in the naves, and he plucked a towel off the arm of one of those youths saying, "Oh, excuse me, I forgot mine. Thanks!" The youth was indeed too busy to reply or care, and John Luke pretended to be dusting the golden stairs and then the throne itself before he completely disappeared behind it. The throne was almost exactly in front of the inner chamber door. The faithful squire of the prince just unlocked the secret passage and entered, then closed the portal, leaving its mysteries intact. He, in all his humility, was never even noticed.

He made his way to the tapestry on the wall and felt the doorway behind it. Tucking himself under the woven threads, he then started to turn the key inside the lock but realized when he pushed on the handle that the little door was already open. Grateful for this, he commenced his quick descent down a narrow passageway that quite conveniently was already lit. Stone cages were carved along the walls to hold strange bone-white torches and wicks that seemed serene in their burning – no flickers, just a continual flame. "Amazing," John Luke said to himself as he heard his heart pumping, but at the bottom of the staircase his poor heart stopped. There in front of him sat the king of Heartland reading a manuscript.

"Oh! So you've come to me, yeh boy!" The king smirked, looking up at the youth. "I knew that old monk-priest and traitor to my cause had a spare key! And what of that protrusion from your chest?"

The King waited for a long moment and then laughed as he managed to lift his rotund body out of the chair and lean on the desk with his huge, fat knuckles. "The cat got your tongue, boy?!" The wide chair arms seemed to catch and stick him to a three-quarter upright position for a moment. That was long enough for John Luke to notice some of the wretched iron implements hanging on the wall and the keys hanging there as well, right where the prince said they would be.

"So, are you siding with my late prince or with me, your king?" asked his majesty rather bluntly as he finally loosened himself and made his way around the desk. He placed his person between the iron implements and John Luke.

"I am siding with Heartland, sir," said the youth brightly.

"Well, what of that?" said the king, noticing the youth shimmying toward a far wall and mistaking it for shyness. "Heartland must side with her king; therefore, you side with me." He was contented with this view but wished to poke at the youth more. For this, he would need another swig of wine; he'd had enough to displace the murder of a martyr from his mind this morning and the loss of a treacherous son. One more swig and this youth would come to his senses for sure. "Everybody seems to be making their final choices today, my boy," said the king as he turned his back to the youth, walked over to the other side of the desk, and picked up a flask of drink. "It's too bad you are so young – how many years do you have? Fifteen?" As the king swirled around with his dreg, he came face-to-face with a fifteen-year-old youth and a jagged-edged iron instrument that had a hinge in the center of it which opened and closed around the neck area of a victim.

"Sir, in the name of Jesus Christ of Nazareth, do not make me use this thing. I implore you, in the name of God's holy mercies to let Jacob go! He is innocent and you know he is!" John Luke was shaking uncontrollably.

"Now, now boy! Put that thing down. I won't hurt you. As for Jacob, he is, amazingly enough, still alive. They must make those Jews from Venice out of velvet and iron! I couldn't even bust his joints ... yet."

The instrument fell to the floor; John Luke was overcome by the king's heinous, sinful nature, which had been given full grounds to develop in his personage and by his own free will. John Luke knew that this man, as he was, would never listen to reason. Getting to Jacob was beyond him; he just started to pray silently to the Lord for help.

"Never let a boy do a man's job!" shouted the criminal capped with a crown. Seeing the youth's fearful hesitation mixed with too much mercy that often lingers in children, he added, "Now, I'll have to finish you off, boy! I think you've sided with my late son!" He came upon John Luke and turned him around like a twirling leaf falling from a tree and wrapped his arms through the youth's arms so his hands were up against John Luke's head. "It's time to cap you, boy!"

Before John Luke's head could make its first forced contact with the stone wall in front of him, the smart young knight in the small boy came to, and using the unsteady drunkenness of the rotund king, he balanced on one leg and then the other to cause the king to wobble. Thus taking him by complete surprise, the youth lurched slightly forward, still on one side, and then hurled his much smaller body back onto the king's, which caused the old, fat fiend to totally lose his balance and fall down flat on the stone floor, back first!

"Haaaa!" The scream that the wicked royal made was pathetic, but could probably be heard by the gentry already at table feasting at his command and awaiting his presence. John Luke, already loosened because of his opponent's pain, got himself up and just looked down at him, stating in a timid fury, "I must go now, sir!"

"Haaaa!" was all the king could say, in a pain and a torment that he had never yet succumbed to in all of his life; he could not even speak or move as he was temporarily paralyzed up and down all of his back. When the guards opened the other door to the dungeon to come in, obviously having heard the screams, John Luke hid behind its hinges and skirted out the door once they were all encircled around their lord with their backs to John Luke. The king could not even lift his hand to point to his young adversary or say a word against him.

"John Luke!" The squire heard a loud shout as he ran past an open cell. The bars were splayed wide open, and he entered quickly to find Jacob. His hands and feet were attached by hemp and iron chains to each corner of a repulsive wooden device.

John Luke realized instantly that he forgot to visit Paul the blacksmith. He panicked. "What do I do! I have no knife!"

"Get me out of this thing! Cut the hemp! They used that instead of the iron shackles to continuously cut my circulation. Look in the corner there – there's a big one!" shouted Jacob, turning his head to a small wooden table located at the far corner on the left. On top of it, many knives were waiting some abominable sinister spoil. "God forestalled their horrible secret plans somehow! Hurry up! I've been partially feigning back misery all morning!" confessed the persecuted man.

"What do you mean?" asked John Luke as he cut the hemp.

"The wooden latch in the middle of this thing must have broken with somebody else. The poor wretch. At any rate, it is a miracle those drunken idiots did not recognize that this frame was not extending." As John Luke helped Jacob out of the killer's cradle, they both looked down and saw the broken latch.

"This way, please ... hurry!" stated a man at the door of the cell. Jacob and John Luke looked up in sudden shock, thinking they had been discovered, but they saw an old hermit instead with torture marks on his hands and feet. "I know this area of the castle all too well, gentlemen. Follow me."

Chapter 10;

One of the Master Craftsmen, a Serf, and a Mythical Bridge Made to Serve Reality

The old hermit took them through a maze of cells until they arrived at a parallel hallway to the one John Luke first ran down when he came to rescue Jacob. "This must be the other side of the castle near the guards' entrance," stated John Luke.

"Yes," acknowledged the hermit, "but there won't be any guards there, just as there were none in Jacob's cell with the door wide open. They all flew to their lord's succor the moment they heard him scream as if he were already in hell."

"If he doesn't repent and change his ways," said John Luke, "I fear that place is just where he will be for eternity."

"I must agree wholeheartedly," said Jacob with utmost confidence. The old hermit turned to him and smiled empathetically as he took the man's shoulder to both guide and lean on him.

"I mean, I do hope he does change, of course." Jacob said this only for the youth, but as he looked into the old hermit's eyes, he saw a paternal love that was the nearest thing to perfect understanding that he had ever seen. Such old eyes filled with love and joy for him. Did he know the old man? It seemed that the hermit had lived through much more pain than he. Jacob saw in those eyes a broken latch. His substitute, the man who went before him. But how could this be? Surely no one could live through torture like that? However, before he could say anything to the old man, he spoke. "Those are the doors to walk through." The old hermit pointed them out to both men. He let go of Jacob's shoulder as the man walked forward with John Luke at his other side. Opening up the heavy, iron-framed wooden doors, both men looked back as Jacob said, "Aren't you coming with us?"

They both gasped; there was no one there.

Like ghosts coming into the light, the two men walked out to freedom in a perplexed joy.

"We saw the Angel of the Lord, Jacob, and we still live," were John Luke's only words.

Jacob had no more tears for sorrow nor for glee; what he did have was a final peace and a terrible confidence that the God of Israel loved him beyond measure, beyond limb and life itself.

Mark and Gregory were about to end their tree romp when they noticed these ghosts of the Lord.

"My God!" shouted Mark in shocked awe. "It's them! Let's go!" Simultaneously, in a boy's second, they both jumped out of the tree. Both parties met, went to the small door in the wall, and John Luke opened it; it had never been locked.

"God doesn't share his mysteries with fools," said John Luke, still dazed by the prior meeting.

"And fools never find out because they trip on what they presume to be illusionary!" added Jacob, smiling.

"What happened to you two?" asked Gregory. "You look like you've seen a gh – " He stopped short as he saw the lassos ready to be thrown in front of him when he walked through the door. He also saw the folded-up bridge as John Luke shut the door. "I don't believe this! I am looking right at it, and I still don't believe it!" he confessed.

"Maybe Mark can convince you when he lassos the polls across the moat," said John Luke, smiling.

"This should be easier because they are not moving." Mark moved quickly with the lassos as he opened the opposing door from which the bridge would unfold. He did his part in record time; being at the luncheon with the ladies, the sentries never noticed the perfection of his craft. He and Jacob started pulling at the separate ropes attached and the bridge started coming forth. John Luke and Gregory secured the staying end of the bridge with twin iron hooks thrown over the securing polls. "It is even easier with four men than three," said Gregory to Jacob, smiling at the freedom he felt inside himself and saw in Jacob's eyes.

The four men walked over the bridge, fleet of step, and went to the peasant huts. Inside the old hemp maker's hut, Jacob found him on his bed in a babe's position. He awoke the old man, over-tired from grief and bereft agony, and told the whole story of his capture and his rescue. They realized that they could not stay with him or any of the few peasants who were now left still working in the fields after such a tragic morning; their presence alone put the poor serfs in danger. The party instead decided to find Prince Peter, if he was still alive, and rescue the maids. After a short stay with Cassandra's father, who was brought back to life again by the kindness and bravery of true friends, the foursome thanked him profusely for making a most excellent bridge. Since the "illusionary fantasy" was still up and would soon be discovered as real, the five minds mused and came up with a dreamlike story to tell any wicked authority, should they come and ask.

"Since none of the others have seen you four," said the wily hemp master, "I will deny its existence at first. Then, if they force me to see it, I will say that Rogenshire knights must have come, placed it there, and captured Jacob because they wanted all his treasures."

"It is a good plan," said Jacob. "After all, they have denied the existence of it up until this very hour, and knowing them, they hopefully will be too ignorant to realize that it had to have started from the inner wall not the outer wall because of the way it was made."

"I'm sorry that Paul and I never invented it to roll up both ways, my friends. However, the prince used it on occasion to flee the castle for a time for himself, for others, and, as of late, to see Cassandra. Brother Barnabas would often leave with him to take care of the rest of us outside the wall. I would often accompany them back into the castle, and our monk would hide me in the sanctuary rooms until I could mill about with the crowd and leave the castle via the drawbridge amid the people and the tradesmen. I never thought to have our secret bridge roll up any other way. He would always return to his father's abuses. The returns were never for him, obviously, only for Heartland." The worn-out serf spoke more like a master tradesman once again.

"Well, Godspeed to you, sir," said John Luke. "We must be getting on as time is very short." Suddenly remembering that he had it, John Luke gave Jacob back his monocular. "It seemed to have stuck to my chest, good fellow," he explained to Jacob. All of them laughed, bid a fond farewell to Cassandra's father with a hug and a kiss on the neck, and followed Jacob out of the hut and into the foreboding forest.

"Prince Peter has your maps, Jacob," said John Luke forlornly.

"Do not worry yourself, John Luke, I know this forest in the biblical way," he admitted, smiling. "Hopefully, the prince will be taking the short route to Rogenshire, which will pass him right by my lady's house."

"You have a lady here?" said Gregory, surprised.

"He's joking, silly," said Mark. "The only house from here that I have heard my master knight talk about on the short route to Rogenshire belongs to a hag."

Jacob just smiled.

Chapter II:

The Serf Maids to Be Found

It had already become midmorning since Montgomery galloped across the small rear drawbridge and into the forest path at lightning speed to be swallowed up by the thick, black forest. Both steed and sovereign then took a much less frequented path filled with endless, monotonous steps of drudgery on Montgomery's part. The prince had to hack away branch after branch, and after traveling due north they came upon the short route to Rogenshire, which was due east. Looking to their right, they noticed a sign which said, "DO NOT ENTER," pointing directly to the path from whence they had just come!

"Oh well, so much for warnings!" chuckled Prince Peter on his steed. Montgomery rolled his eyes, realizing that his prince had never really looked at the maps prior to now. The steed started to pull fresh blades of grass from one spot in the ground near an oak tree, while Prince Peter pulled out Jacob's maps and looked over the geography of his beloved Heartland. There was a river flowing from his kingdom and a few paths that led through the forest in different directions. One of the largest was a wide road which was built on top of the old Roman road used by many because it linked all of the kingdoms. It even led down to the great sea and passed through the Frankish kingdom on the opposite coast and eventually led to Rome, so the Prince was told. "Jacob comes from a place called Venice which must be somewhere on the main continent." He then added, as if Montgomery couldn't tell, "I've never yet been."

Looking long and hard while Montgomery munched, the prince spoke. "Well, Montgomery, Heartland is very well represented here with detailed information about our gentry's residences of good standing and quality buying. There is the yard as well, where we have our May celebration and the fair. Jacob has put an "X" on the spot where he rents the extra house Paul the blacksmith has near the central fountain. I have seen the wonderful books and trappings of luxury in that house. Paul keeps it for Jacob all year round."

Montgomery whinnied. He wished that there would be no interruption while he was eating. His wish was not granted. His master kept talking. "There are spots of interest with the forest dwellers, too ... an inn on this road, it seems. We can go there and inquire. Chances are, the rogues who have my Cassandra and the others may pass by that very place."

Montgomery whinnied loud and long. His nostrils flared and he got a little agitated. Prince Peter thought nothing about it as he looked over the Heartland forest section of the map. It contained an outline of an inn and a smaller path that intercepted the short trail, which eventually found either the back road or the Roman road from Heartland. "Hah, yes!" mused Prince Peter to himself as Montgomery semi-pranced in a standing position. "Jacob actually found a tiny path that intercepts both the long and the short paths around my kingdom. This must be the path we just took. Ha! Yes! Now I see the 'DO NOT ENTER' sign!"

Montgomery rolled his eyes and snorted as his master continued, "It looks so convenient ... Montgomery, do you smell fire or something? What's wrong?"

The horse began to whinny uncontrollably and when the poor steed looked up at the sky, he just rolled his eyes again and shook his head back and forth. It was then that Prince Peter could almost smell something burning in the air, but the forest was so thick he could not yet see smoke. Looking up through the leaves in the trees to the sky, he saw ominous black clouds gathering. "Let us go, Montgomery," said brave Prince Peter, stuffing Jacob's maps back underneath his gambeson wool, which was under his chain mail and breastplate. "If into a fire we fade, then we'll come out the other side with the rain as our shield and shade!"

The marvelous stallion whinnied a stout agreement and obeyed the prince's shout to gallop with the haste, strength, and courage of a faithful destrier.

Smoke filled Montgomery's nostrils as he galloped; he kept his course, snorting the stuff out of his long snout, refusing to stop. As the evil, transparent gray veil enveloped them, they saw a huge black funnel of smoke rising fast when they came upon a disastrous situation. "This must be the inn, my friend!" shouted the prince to his steed.

Montgomery gave a short whinny and snorted continuously as the gold spurs hit his sides once. The faithful steed felt like stopping completely short at that moment; he hated spurs, gold or otherwise. However, believing that someone needed them both, he kept up the rapid speed. He looked up for a moment and saw the sky start to rain down upon him. Relief from the polluted air came in due course as the strong stream of rain poured down upon horse and rider. Montgomery arrived at the scene of devastation with the prince still atop him, seemingly too late. The reddish hue in the atmosphere died down eventually as Montgomery just stood there, catching his breath in mad disappointment. As the gray mist dispersed, master and horse were able to see the carnage. They both gazed at the wreck of a house with the rain pelting down inside a hole with an iron circular staircase. The hole and the staircase were the only structures left totally intact.

"Well," said Prince Peter to his steed with more than a bit of distain in his voice, "guess who passed here recently!"

Montgomery whinnied with a short moan of understanding as he tousled his head again, his mane wafting in the gray breeze. His master dismounted and walked up to the hole. Iron foot met with iron stair and a *clank, clank, clank* could be heard as Prince Peter descended. What he found was quite enchanting. "Montgomery," he shouted happily up to his steed, "the poor proprietor of this inn was extremely educated! These books are so rained on that the flames in their ignorance overlooked them! I see a solid oak table, still intact, and a beautiful stone fireplace."

Suddenly the fireplace began to move. Startled, Prince Peter unsheathed his sword carefully; the oak table took up most of the space!

When a wrinkled woman appeared in the fireplace, the prince was on the other side of the oak; he thought he was seeing an apparition. She laughed uncontrollably as old hags often do, and said, "Don't worry, fair Prince of Heartland! It is only me, your humble servant."

"It is good to see that you are still alive!" said the prince. "But I had no idea you could appear and reappear. You ought to really ask the Good Lord about that. I don't know if it is that much in line with Scripture."

Not wanting to give Jacob's invention away, she played her part. "I surely will, sire. He is the most beloved King of all. You should not stay here, though, with your steed. You are in danger. The thieves of Rogenshire will return. I have their treasure safe with me."

"Where are they?!" shouted the prince. Having sheathed his sword, he quickly walked over to the woman and grabbed her shoulders just a bit. "Have they been harmed at all?"

"No! Not a bit, fine prince. There is no need to worry." Then she continued, bending at the elbows and putting her long, rough, knobby fingers on the prince's gentle but firm grip. He felt a matronly love pass from them, and it gave him an assurance that she was being truthful with him. "They are in my secret hiding place. But you must leave at once! The fire might attract the dragon from Rogenshire, and it would be a pity if – "

"But they are my responsibility!" protested the prince. "It is I who should return them to Heartland!"

"Return them to a place where they will serve a wicked king in abject bondage until they age faster than even I have and die in the fields?" explained the old hag. "However, that, my dear knight, is not nearly as bad as what was in store for them at Rogenshire. Either way, they must *not* return. Listen to me. I have a plan for all of us!"

"What plan?" asked the knight, both baffled and stunned at the woman's candor about the situation. He kept looking into her eyes, and as close as he was, his mind went beyond her aged, wrinkled face. Her soul seemed so familiar ...

Chapter 12:

Grace, Queen Regent

"I am about to shock you even more, and all too quickly," stated the wise one, still in Peter's grasp. As he stared at her, she admitted in a whisper, as if she no longer believed it herself, "I am your older cousin, Peter, the Princess Grace of what is now Rogenshire – what was once Faithland."

"Before your ancestors lost faith – *Grace*!" He finished the thoughts of his cousin and lifted her head with his forefinger, as it had bowed low at the remembrance of deposition and banishment. "Grace, I thought you were dead! They said you had died during battle with a dragon!"

"Guess what 'they' might or probably have said about you by now, young cousin. The only evil dragons in these parts are the evil thoughts of wicked men and the plans they make, not necessarily against us, but against the Almighty Himself."

The fireplace turned again and Cassandra and Tirzah appeared. "Cassandra!" The Prince took her in his arms with a long, precious kiss. His mind had finally figured out that the fireplace was a wonderful work in mechanics, but the kiss got in the way of his rightful recognition to his cousin. She and Tirzah stood opposite each other with broad smiles – one with pearls of white and the other with the memory of them. This bliss lasted a long moment.

"Cousin, we have no time!" shouted Grace as she heard the warning whinny of Montgomery.

The prince looked upon her again. "What, Princess Grace – how can I help you regain your throne and take what rightfully belongs to me and mine for the heart of Heartland?"

"Our thrones, cousin, God will bestow upon us only if we take proper care of the poor, not keep them that way but teach them and raise them up. These innocent, right now, are our poor. We ourselves are now also poor. God is the only rich kindred Redeemer, and it is His plan I have."

"Oh, this is such old Christian thinking, but I so long for it; whether I live in it or die for it, I care not. God will make that choice. His plan, Grace. What say you?" Peter, filled with enthusiasm and the acknowledgement of Grace's kindred spirit, listened well to the wisdom.

"Good. Let us work on keeping God's throne of *love* in the hearts of humanity first, cousin. Then, He may bend down far to the dust of the earth to set us both aright."

"Is it outrageous to war, then?" asked the prince with somewhat of a whine. He was tired of fighting; even though he was very fine at it, he'd been doing it his whole short life.

"It is good only in defense of self and the helpless. I pray that if we make a few mistakes along the way, that God Himself remembers that He is the only perfect One!" Peter chuckled at that but Grace was deadly serious as she pulled a long sheath from behind a bookcase. "This is my sword; I can no longer wield it as my arms pain me when I move them certain ways. I know not what it is and my herbs give me only brief relief."

She gave him a beautiful, double-edged, deadly work of art; the hilt gleamed its golden entwined and circular barrier with the handle emblazoned with "gRf," which stood for "Grace Queen Regent of Faithland," on one side and her old family crest of the fox and the stag on the other side.

"This was made for my coronation that never took place after father's mysterious death," said Grace mournfully. "You are ambidextrous, as I remember, young cousin; be as cunning as the fox, for the dogs are now on the hunt. Succeed and the mighty years of prosperity and strength will abound to you as the stag in a well-kept forest. Go now and allow yourself and your mighty friend to be the decoys on the forbidden path. You will have to turn around and go south for a moment, but turn left at the sign – "

"I remember it," said Peter. "I passed it coming out of a small path. We had just come out of the place with the sign that said 'DO NOT ENTER.'" Montgomery, listening from the top stair, whinnied a happy assurance for his master but, as no one was looking, he rolled his eyes. He remembered that same path all too well from the whole morning and wasn't so sure that this idea of his master's cousin was a profitable one. Nonetheless, he would obey, knowing, as all faithful steeds do, that he could think while on course; he was a warhorse.

"When you turn onto the path at your left, it will lead you southward, and then there will be a left turn in the road. Take it; the road runs parallel to this side road, and after a slow walk on your steed – unless you are being followed by the rogues of Rogenshire – after a half day's journey, you will come to the mouth of the underground river which encircles my father's old castle. My wicked younger brother, now enthroned, is building a new type of castle around my family's old one. Unfortunately, its foundations are on the top of the lake's ground ceiling. The earth is not thick in these areas; this is the very reason for the original castle's dimensions. In all his arrogance, my wicked sibling doesn't realize this. He also doesn't know that he is building atop the Rogenshire dragon's home – if she still exists.

"What do I do then? Why should I move right into a dragon's lair? Will the serfs in the fields see me at some point if I move parallel to this road? Why must I be a decoy in the first place? Why is this path so forbidden?"

Before the princess could answer any of his questions, Montgomery went from another whinny to an outright declarative neigh.

"Go! Do as I say and stay on your horse! Never get off!" She rushed him up the iron staircase, taking the sword as Montgomery actually lay down so his master could get atop him quickly. Princess Grace helped him balance as Montgomery arose and gave Prince Peter her sheath and sword. He held the reins with one hand and his new equipment in the other as the horse galloped off just in time to distance themselves between the wicked and the dismal carnage. Montgomery stopped and gave a very loud whinny as his Lord Prince shouted rather loudly, "The fox wants to be hunted again, Montgomery! This fox sides with righteousness! We'll see who wins! The wicked or the willing!" The condemned souls in armor bought the bait and looked to follow him whom they thought stole their prey. As they looked the wrong way, Princess Grace and the two young maidens returned themselves again into safety and rested behind the ashes.

Chapter 13:

Paul the Blacksmith is Also the Giant King of the Forest

Walking through the forest from the back field nearest the castle wall, Jacob and the three youths found a river and started to follow it. "This leads to the Rogenshire Castle and actually goes underground. I know an underground entrance right into the castle; it is a trap door that opens up into the paymaster's chambers."

"You know the paymaster?" asked Gregory.

Following Jacob to the river, they all lay down by the banks and scooped up some clear, cool drink.

"I knew the old one, when Grace was still at her post," Jacob stated, not realizing he gave away a secret.

"Grace ... ," John Luke mused out loud. After they arose and walked a small path that ran along the bank, John Luke still thought. Suddenly, as if from the dead, he remembered a onetime story he had been told about a beautiful yet banished Grace and exclaimed with a questioning shout, "Grace ... Princess Grace of Rogenshire?"

"Be quiet!" stated Jacob with a firm look at John Luke. "We are walking in hopeful anonymity. I don't want to be found out by the forest dwellers." He could have kicked himself for being so loose of tongue. He had kept her secret, at her request, for years. Jacob realized he had become too trusting with too innocent a youth who had helped to save his life. He threw himself into silence.

"But I thought she was dead?" continued John Luke.

Mark pitched in, putting two and two together, "If she is still alive, would she be the lady of the inn?"

Jacob said nothing. Maybe her secret was not a secret after all.

The youths continued to jabber as the forest started to rustle. Jacob did not pay attention as his closed mouth took up all his concentration. However, when he heard the young men's concerns about the prince meeting the dragon, he responded, "Prince Peter will fight the dragon if he is met and he will surely have much with which to succeed. Your concern should be to help him with the wicked knights. Our plan should be to get to the short road, in any case. We are on foot and without horses or even donkeys it will take us – "

"It will take you more than a whole day's journey already, taking this coiled path along my river bank," interrupted a deep, full-throated voice from one of the forest's thick-leaved trees.

"Master Paul!" shouted Gregory, looking frantically toward the sound of the voice. "Yes, master blacksmith, or should I say, 'King of the Forest?'"

Paul the blacksmith chuckled as his giant form emerged from the green blanket of trees. As he caught up and trotted along next to Jacob, he humbly put his huge muscular hands in his side pockets and his head down, looking at the path. "Gregory and the forest folk call me that. It means nothing really – pay no mind to him."

"No, master Paul! You can trust Jacob! He has got to know," pleaded Gregory, running up to the side of the walking "oak." John Luke and Mark stared at each other as they walked behind the others, but Jacob only pretended confusion. "Now, Gregory. We all know Paul here is not your master – you just call him that out of respect and high regard."

"High indeed, sir!" agreed Gregory, pretending to bow to a high lord of good standing as they all tittered.

"Well, I guess I can confide in you, stranger, since you are in and out of these lands on a regular basis. The forest folk don't consider you a stranger at all, though. They like you, Jacob," the forest king added, "and if they like you, and they like hiding you at times from cowards and thieves, well then, so must I." Paul patted Jacob on the back.

"I must say," said Jacob, "I can't reward them enough for safe passage. The life of my daughter means more to me than anything I could ever give … "

"I know, Jacob," said Paul meekly. "We thank you for teaching us about the world outside of this forest, outside of these kingdoms, and even this huge island, but don't fret about Tirzah. She was caught by your gracious love and they have made it to our camp. They are all safe."

"What and thank you!" shouted Jacob, stopping his stride and the giant by one arm. "How did 'we' manage this, and how do you know that the innkeeper is my lady love?"

Paul just smiled and winked. He had never revealed secrets in the past and was not about to start now, even with half of the secret himself. He just answered the first part of Jacob's question. "After the rogues burned the house down, your hiding place was used by our lady at the inn, but her tunnel attached to the space you created caved in with the rain. Fortunately, Prince Peter came along, God bless him. He used himself as a decoy, and as soon as the hounds followed him onto the forbidden path, your lady and friends were able to escape into the southeast woods from Rogenshire, or the middle woods between both kingdoms. They made it to our camp soon enough," said the forest giant.

"Thank goodness." Jacob bent down, putting his hands on his knees. His bangs fell in front of his face; he caught his breath with more than a few sighs of relief. The others rested as well, but the moment of peace was brief. They heard horse hooves in the distance on the path. Branches were being hacked away at an ungodly rate of speed.

"Quickly, we don't have far to go!" whispered Paul as Jacob straightened himself out in a heartbeat, whisking his hair back on his head and shepherding the young youths toward the forest entrance. Just as the entourage of knights fleeted down the back path, the forest king and his friends slipped through a leaved entrance way, their "door" falling down to the green floor beneath them as a blanket of woven vines and ferns purposefully yet naturally entangled together. They were never seen but could see everything that passed. "They were not looking for us," said Gregory with a sigh of relief. Climbing the tall tree to which the "stage curtain" was attached, Mark viewed those passing without a word. Everyone waited for his report. The final short jump to the ground after a wonderful show of his acrobatic talents started the tale of good news. "Gregory's hunch is right. They are not following us at all. There is a one-man cart in the middle of that band with the king of Heartland in it. He must be in pain because he is flat on his back surrounded by pillows and blankets. The bustling must ache him terribly. They must be going to the kingdom south of us where the surgeon is located."

"They are going to open him up!" shouted John Luke with no fear since the entourage had long since disappeared. "That is hardly ever done! Oh my. I think I've done it. I didn't mean to, you know ... it's just that – "

"What happened, my friend, before you got to me?" asked Jacob with a total smile from ear to ear. Not a one, really, was without a smile, although they tried to hide their glee for he was a king, as wicked as he was. John Luke related his endeavors to the group as they walked to the camp. Everyone realized that the king would really need that surgeon! Paul said that his entourage probably took one of the smaller paths because the king might not have wanted his populace to realize what desperate a state he was in, indeed.

Talk and plans ensued about getting to Prince Peter; to help a prince who made himself a substitute for a lady was a very fine thing, and a very right thing to do. They all realized that God just may be planning a coup d'etat for Himself. To have good win over evil and breathe one day of freedom– just one day, never mind a whole lifetime of freedom – the forest king and his friends all agreed was a day worth fighting for and even a day worth dying for.

"Oh, Jacob," stated Paul as he gave the man a goodly slap on the back while they walked through the forest following a small river that wound through the middle of it, "you have to admit, life here in these northern lands is never boring!"

"Indeed it is not!" laughed Jacob.

"I say," added Paul, "how many men are struck by the iron gauntlet, racked, rescued, walked over a bridge that is supposed to be illusionary, and get kidnapped by the forest king all in one day?"

"Kidnapped?" shouted John Luke.

"Well, if he doesn't have his clothes, his products, his maps, his wife, his daughter, or his life to himself, what would you call that, John Luke?" stated Paul.

"Kidnapped ever so kindly?" The youth smirked. They all laughed at that as they came to what appeared to be the end of the path along the river. Gregory went behind a huge oak tree in front of the "dead end" and seemed to be pulling down on some hemp. As he pulled, another "natural curtain" arose. The stage was set. Jacob was not able to see inside, but Tirzah had already seen him from the other side of the curtain and was running to him. He had made it to the forest camp. The only things that remained missing from him were his maps and the life of Tirzah's substitute. He drew her close to his chest, kissed the top of her beautiful auburn head, and realized that he had to fight with these people who desperately needed their kingdom back.

Chapter 14;

The Errant Knight is Lost Yet Found

Whacking and hacking through the extremely small path from which he had practically just come, the errant knight was so tempted to just get off his horse and struggle more slowly but, as warned by the princess, he could not do so. The evil hounds were on his trail; they were hacking just as much as he, as if the vines and leaves of the forest regrew in miraculous moments, wanting to keep a secret completely and totally hidden. At one point, when the prince's arms were about to fall off from dire fatigue, a tiny path to his left was lit by rays of the sun, and only for a moment. Montgomery saw it too and took it immediately. His hooves were in pain from some of the small rocks along the very rough trail. He was thankful that armor was put on his head and his whole body because the brambles he had been literally pushing aside would have caused him much cutting and blood loss all throughout the morning, but especially now, since a much faster speed had to be maintained. Montgomery smelled an air of peace as soon as he turned into a part of the tiny road. The brambles closed behind them immediately and they walked a small distance and stopped. Neither one made a sound as Montgomery's haunches were very near a strange part of the forbidden path which they did not remember passing by before. Fortunately, the duo were completely safe and were not heard nor seen by their hunters, who passed right by them. Waiting for a moment, and soaking in the peace, they looked in front and all around them. The two blond-haired warriors noticed how the air seemed to be filled with a rainbow light as lingering drops of water on elegantly-veined leaves glittered like diamonds in a pinkish-purple mist and rays of sunlight gleamed through the green shade. Walking ever so slowly, recuperating from all the morning's events, Montgomery and his rider came upon a small stream. He immediately bowed his head to drink. The steed was so thirsty, he forgot his master who still sat upon him.

Suddenly, an old hermit appeared from beneath a miniature stone bridge to their left that crossed the small stream. "Let me help you off your horse, my prince," said the old one.

"No," stated the prince, remembering the princess' warning. However, Montgomery lifted his muscular neck from the river and gave a joyful whinny signifying that all was fine; this man could be completely trusted. The horse smelled an abundant peace and compassion all around this hermit. Montgomery knew as soon as he had entered the domain that the hidden ambiance of love and peace was all because of this elderly man.

"Oh," expressed the prince at the "remark" of his destrier. "My noble steed seems to trust you implicitly," he continued, trying to get off the horse on his own. Montgomery stopped drinking and bent his forelegs down and then his aft. The old hermit helped the armored champion off the horse's huge back and threw off all the horse's armor with astonishing strength. He placed all the destrier's equipage under a large, luxuriously-leaved and multicolored bush; the flowers thereof seemed to dance with delight at the job of hiding the tools of righteousness where absolutely no soul would ever notice their presence. The faithful animal was finally free to bask in the mild heat of the sun's rays; the brilliant blond lights in his mane twinkled back the yellow-and-pink lights as soon as they alit themselves upon its thick glamour.

The hermit helped the prince take off his armor and walked ahead of him to set it under the stone bridge along a wide ledge near a little wooden door. As he approached the bridge, the prince noticed a strange white smoke coming from the stump of a chopped pine tree on the little knoll just beyond the little wooden door. The little door and the ledge were just about three paces above the riverbank under the bridge, and after the old man opened the door, Prince Peter found himself in a small stone chamber; there was a door at the other end which faced the back domain of this part of the forest. It looked toward the very way to the short road that led to Rogenshire. Inside the underground hut there existed a very small table and two knotted chairs, all of which were made of a pine wood. There was even a little stone fireplace with an iron kettle and a fire going. Mint tea had already been prepared and a meal of rabbits and home garden vegetables was waiting to be eaten. There was a wooden jar with honey on the table along with plates, knives, and spoons, all made of wood. Prince Peter also noticed a small wooden bed with hay atop it. A lamb's skin was the blanket of choice for this hermit. All the wool must have kept him warm during the cold nights.

"Please sit down and allow me to serve you, my prince," said the old man, taking his apron and putting it on. With some fresh, warm water by the fire and a flask of some very expensive oil, he knelt down in front of the chair he wished the prince to sit on because he was ready to wash his sore feet. "Oh, no," stated the prince firmly, "there is no need to do this." He still sat down in exhaustion.

The old man poured out the water and ran the oil over the prince's foot. The whole royal person melted in the wooden chair and slouched in spent relaxation. "Your feet, my dear young man, do not smell like roses!"

All the Prince could do was laugh mildly. "Thank you, sir, but why do you call me, 'my prince'? Are you not a member of the forest dwellers? I do not know you."

"Hah! But you are my prince and have known me all your short life. You have been very faithful to me, indeed," said the old hermit as he finished his deed of service to the royal's feet. Poor Prince Peter thought the old man a very good-hearted, senile fellow who had lived out in nature way too long. When the old man began serving him his own rabbit stew, he thought that something terrible must have happened to him at some point to lose his mind so. "*Maybe he lost a son,"* he mused as he gratefully dipped the well-used wooden spoon into a flavorful brew of thick-spiced meat and vegetables. The meat was so tender no knife of any kind was needed. Another bucket of warm water had been by the fire, and the prince eyed it as he fixed his plate, thinking the old man must have purposed it for his own bath. There was just enough stew for two, as if the prince had sent a messenger in advance to let the old man know he was coming! *"How odd,"* thought the prince, when the hermit kept a continuous timid smile on his face. *"Can he read my thoughts?"*

At that thought, the old hermit looked over at him from the fireplace but said nothing; his eyes twinkled. He placed his own plate at the table and went back to retrieve the second bucket of water; he picked that up and brought it over to the table. Tipping the bucket ever so gently, he poured fresh, warm, deep red wine out into the wooden goblets! When he put the bucket down, red wine was inside. Now the prince was in shock; he picked up his goblet – the hermit had already taken a small swallow of his own – and tasted the substance. It had a smooth, deep, burly, barky, berry flavor. It wasn't sweet as much as it was strong and oak solid. It was the best wine he'd ever tasted in his life!

Chapter 15:

Uncommon Confessions and Noble Loyalty in the Wild

Jacob was led by his daughter's hand to a cedar house well hidden in the camp confinement, the whole camp mysteriously covered by groups of hempen and wooden pulley "walls" of woven leaves and vines. Tirzah told him, "The folks here told me that the first man to leave Rogenshire came here via an old hermit; he showed him how to build the walls. The only thing the man regretted before he died was the fact that the walls were only mechanical. The folks who followed him from both kingdoms as time went on still couldn't figure out what he meant by that."

Jacob just smiled. He was invited into the maidens' house, as he was the father of one of them. When everyone feasted, Tirzah went back to join them so there was no maiden present save for the withered but spirit-strong Grace lying down on one of the many straw beds. Bending down on one knee, Jacob wrapped his long-time lover in the embrace of his still-strong arms. She awoke to see his eyes shining down upon her. "My dear Jacob," she whispered adoringly, her forefinger touching his chapped lips. "I have left our young cousin-prince in danger; it is tragic but the maids ..." she just kept musing with a furrowed brow.

"I know. Grace, the decision was a good one; however, I am obligated to try to find and help him." Jacob finished the phrase for her and added an ending with which she did not agree.

"No, you are not!" she shouted, having heaved up some sort of energy from years long gone. It sprouted up from a hidden part within her; she could not suppress it. She tried to get up but Jacob kept her from doing so; his body and his mind were about to quarrel with her and make his point.

"Yes I am," he stated quite firmly. "One of those young ladies happens to be my daughter. The obligation is all mine. I will find him."

"I made him take the route!" admitted Grace just as firmly, but lacked the ability to move on her decision because of Jacob's embrace.

"We may stay here all day and quarrel over this situation, my love, but you are staying here and I am leaving!" insisted the merchant, adventurer, teacher, and mason.

"No, I am not staying here!" shouted Grace, the royal warrior.

"How can you leave when I am holding you in loving captivity?" Jacob chuckled. Although fatigued, he still thought himself the logical one.

"As soon as you get up and leave I am following you, Jacob Santoro!" she quickly rebuffed him, and he was astonished at her revived spirit. After a long kiss, he reluctantly got up, succumbing to her, and they both packed a sword for Jacob, knives, and a dragon lantern for their journey.

"The forbidden path leads to one of the old dragon's lairs straight away and near the southern fields of Heartland," stated Grace as she ate a little of the meat and berries that had been brought to her prior. Jacob also ate some nourishment; there was plenty provided.

"Yes, but as of recent, all the peasants work the north fields on the other side of the castle," said Jacob. "That's how the young squires and I got on the other trail so quickly. We took the middle hidden entrance used by the peasantry."

"And the fleeing forest folk," said Grace.

"Yes," said Jacob, still chortling, "and the fleeing forest folk who have giants with bodies and hearts just as big to help them hither and yon!" Jacob and Grace both smiled.

"Paul found you on the road, then?" she asked.

"Yes, and the injured king and his men on horses flew past us on that same trail as we entered Paul's lair here. Did you hear John Luke's story?" asked Jacob to his princess.

"I obviously did not hear it!" she exclaimed excitedly. "Was the king mortally wounded somehow?"

"It just may be so," explained Jacob. "His riders took the small back trail to avoid being noticed, which means they must fly north before they can get to the highway and go once again to the west and south."

"Well and good. Enough of that, we must press on," said Grace.

"I don't think we should go to the old lair," stated Jacob.

"Why not? The forbidden path leads right to it!" Grace reminded her partner. And then she thought, *"Unless he did turn left at one of Paul's paths. Nonetheless, I had no time to explain exactly where that was located."* Grace's confidence turned to a whimper and she stopped packing.

"Firstly, he may not have made it there." Jacob looked down at the dirt floor, not knowing whether good or evil had befallen this hero. Neither one was packing at that moment.

Grace spoke sadly but in a confident tone. "I told him never to dismount. He had a good advantage, and with such an excellent horse, he – "

"No, no, no," interrupted Jacob. "You did not hear my part, my love, and there again for what is your part of this conversation, within that path down which you sent him and Montgomery there have been strange but goodly mysteries as of late, I've been told," explained the teacher with a twinge of hope in his voice.

"Oh," mocked Grace, stuffing her very last provision with complete lack of patience, "you mean a baby dragon converted itself to the good, or maybe his fire doesn't work, or he might have converted to a diet of herbs?" She just looked at him with hand on hip as if he was totally out of his mind.

"All these things could have and may have happened, although I think not," said Jacob matter-of-factly, looking at his lover with imploring, forlorn eyes. He pleaded without words for some mercy but received none. So he was forced to explain a foolish adventure: "Just simply, I checked the old lair upon my return to Heartland and there was no dragon there, no lingering smell of sulfur. The cave where they resided actually had a free flow of fresh air from some underground vent; it smelled like the wild flowers of the field."

Surprisingly, the princess ignored the ignominious task of his curiosity; she was so caught up with finding her cousin, she seemed not to care for the moment. Jacob was relieved and did not interrupt her thoughts.

"So, they have not been there for a long time," answered the princess, standing upright in surprise and respect for her partner but now bent on pondering the next stratagem since her first was now moot.

"If you told him to take the forbidden path as I said," stated her lover, "he might have followed the merging of the old back path to Heartland from the back gate, but that hasn't been used in years and it also passes the dragon cave. Hence, the dragon is no longer there as proved, if, in fact, that was the path he originally took to get to the inn."

"When he first started on his errantry, we don't know which exit of his kingdom he had taken," the princess continued, finger on lips. "But, at this point, he either got back to Heartland or actually took to the left and made it to the fountainhead and the cave of the underground lake of my old kingdom ... "

The princess looked down. Her partner finished the phrase, "Or was made a martyr."

"So," said she frankly, "if he was made a martyr, he is safe in heaven now and it is up to us to punish the perpetrators; if he took the old unused path off the forbidden one having found its mergence, he is at the back gate again in his own kingdom, possibly positioned to take the throne back for righteousness sake. It is most unlikely at a certain point that the rogues from Rogenshire actually would follow him all the way back to his kingdom. However, if he did veer off the path somehow to the left as a few forest folk have as of late, only returning with a healing of a limb or a sickness gone or a peace they never had before, this same good fortune might have happened to our prince."

"Where is there a trail – that wondrous trail which we are all hearing about?" asked Jacob.

"Folks simply have seen the trail to the left as the leaves bent back to meet them … so they say," replied the princess with a shrug of her shoulders.

"You mean the leaves and sticks and vines just … ah … bent back on their very own to meet these blessed few?" asked Jacob, now smiling from ear to ear.

"Why do you smile so? And yes, that is what they have said at my inn; nonetheless, Jacob, I have not yet experienced what they speak of … have you?" the princess questioned him spritely and with a pinch of confusion about her.

"As you will someday hear John Luke's story, you'll have to hear my account as well; they run together," stated the confident teacher once again. This change in attitude seemed flippant and inexplicable to the princess, but she found her mind shaping no words within it for Jacob. Nonetheless, as suddenly as the loss stole her words away from her lips, there popped into her mind's eye a new, focused plan. "We must speed ourselves to the fountainhead. If the brutes are still alive, they would never venture to Heartland so soon because there is practically nothing left in the fields for them to take. They might have stopped chasing our fox for the fear of something on that path that is in love with the downtrodden but hates bullies and brutes and returned to Rogenshire."

"They would never return to their kingdom empty-handed," stated Jacob.

"You are certainly right, my love," said Grace. "They would not dare return empty-handed for fear of losing their positions and their very lives; however, they may, in their dire situation, consider killing the dragon. There is still the adult female, her two children having been killed as of late. I heard that news from Paul. I have also heard that she resides beached under the new part of the castle; Rogenshire peasants can no longer mine because of her. This has been going on for some time. I thought she had traveled from her lair under Rogenshire to her other abode near Heartland. I assumed wrongly; for some reason she no longer commutes from one place to another. There is crystal-clear water there, and she feeds at night. The lake cave at Rogenshire is a perfect place for her. However, she would also be cornered and a perfect alternative gift to my wicked brother," stated Grace with a bit of venom spitting from her mouth.

"You looked just like a dragon when you said that," whispered Jacob. He came close to her and took her two hands in front of his. "My lady, give up your hatred for him, the devil's puppet. The hatred for the devil you may keep." He smiled adoringly at her, and that same smile was returned. Reason was imparted without another word, and they exited the house hand-in-hand and headed for the fountainhead. A quick explanation to Paul and desperate hugs to all were given at one of the "walls" or folded gates to the northeast. Paul declared that he would quietly follow up with his army via the forest.

"To keep you doubly guarded, part of my group will be watching from the most northern part of the underground lake," assured the blacksmith.

"There is no underground opening to the cave that way," declared the princess.

"Oh, my lady," revealed the gentle giant, "as of late my men, whilst they were spying on Rogenshire from a safe distance, noticed that the dragon had actually dug out a vent for herself from the ground up. As for her, she could never squeeze through, so we think. Nonetheless, a human might escape peril or enter danger to save a fellow warrior, which would be, in this case, yourself; we would consider it our honor and duty to serve you, even if it meant to our death."

The princess gasped at the ancient loyalty redeemed from death itself; she felt almost undeserving. It had been so long. She tried to say something, but nothing came out. Jacob broke the silence, "For a forest dweller focused on freedom, you sure do pronounce and act on loyalty with a skilled industry about you!"

"My dear good man," responded Paul, "I will always want the freedom of the wild when the wicked rule, but my heart is to serve righteousness with a reckless abandon. I will always and forever be a traitor to evil; that, my man, is my promise to heaven, and I would rather die in battle than live in cowardice. Both Prince Peter and Queen Grace have my hand and the hands of my forest folk."

The "gate" was lifted up and Jacob escorted his queen out. The last image of Tirzah and Cassandra hugging each other was erased by a lowered wall of leaves and vines as they turned and seemed to walk alone. Jacob did not speak. He was also in a fine, goodly shock. "Queen Grace," they simply whispered together, confirming the words spoken with the thunderous, burly voice that Paul seemed to have been gifted with at his very birth. "From his mouth to the ears of *love*," Queen Grace implored to an eternity much greater than herself as she yearned for the message to come true and her cousin to be alive and safe.

Chapter 16:

The Old King Is Dead! Long Live the King!

"We must be moving along after supper, King Peter," the old hermit whispered to his majesty after they finished their meal and sipped on some tea.

"Oh, excuse me," admonished Peter modestly and with respect, "but I am not a king yet."

"Oh, you most definitely are, my young brave one," challenged the old hermit with a foresight Peter couldn't possibly foresee. "You see, your father was very painfully injured after trying to do much harm to a smaller person. That person, your squire, acted in self-defense. The king's horsemen jostled him in a quick and wicked ride all the way to the king of the south. However, this king had heard of the rebellion of your father and would not help him recover. His surgeons were not permitted to even look upon him. He died in pain and agony, but he did repent of all his evil ways and attitudes. It is amazing what it takes betimes to get people to see their wickedness." He verily whispered the last statement almost to himself.

"But how do you know all this? When did my father's death occur?" questioned Peter, rising up from his chair; his whole visage looked like a perplexed question mark, and he was not at all ready for the response.

"Oh, I have my ways and they are not like yours ... and ... well, as for the last question, within the last five minutes while you were enjoying your relaxed sup with me." The old man looked up at the young, valiant warrior with his cup of tea in hand; he could not hide a smirk and a twinkle in his eye, knowing that the hearts of both father and son, as different as they were, sometimes reacted to the perplexities of life nonetheless very similarly. The twinkle was for Peter, however, because his final decisions and problem-solving abilities were consistently to the good just as much as his father's were to the bad. The hermit chose patience with Peter because of this.

"Oh! I don't know what to say!" exclaimed the new king, although his mind could not yet truly believe what he had heard. "My heart always wanted done with him deep down inside because he continually chose evil against God." The perplexed man looked all around him as if searching for the answer to be on a shelf or the table in front of him. "But I always loved him and would somehow never let go; he was my father. I longed for him to be good."

"So did I, my son," said the hermit. "You have no idea what it feels like to be so rejected, thank goodness."

"What do you mean?" said the servant-son. "I was always rejected by him because of my faith. Oh yes, he was very proud of my accomplishments and thought my acquired skills would bring me closer to his side, but they compelled me to faith instead."

"Why?" asked the senile fellow with a smile before taking a sip.

"Because I found love in every drop of dew, every logical movement mechanisms make, every victory in the hardships of life. My failures or shortcomings only gave me humility. I am quite sure there is someone always with me. A sacrificial love, an eternal Being."

"How do you know this for sure?" said the hermit, putting his wooden cup down on the pine table.

"Because I feel his presence ..." With those last words, Peter's eyes stopped roaming and he looked straight down in front of him. He slowly moved to the old hermit's chair where he was still seated and got down on both knees, just staring eye-to-eye with eternity.

"Welcome home, Peter," said the wise one. "You have been very faithful in small things, now you will have large things. Your squire is safe and your cousin and her husband will win the day for us all." He cupped Peter's head in his old, wrinkled, yet very strong hands.

"I did not know she was married," said Peter.

"Neither does she, yet," chuckled eternity.

Chapter 17:

Deep in Mud and Caught Up to False Skies

The two partners in a coup d'etat walked on a narrow, barely noticed trail which spent itself northeast through the forest and caught up with the stream that became three paces deep at its center and flowed to the mouth of a cave big enough for one man to bend himself through the entrance.

Paul and his army had been covertly following from a furlong circuitously; he did not want to be noticed by any enemy who might approach, yet he wanted to protect "his" couple from any danger from any route. As Jacob entered the mouth of the cave first, a sword in hand, Paul motioned to half of his league to run north atop the land to the new funnel of the dragon. The other half would abide outside for a short span of time, eyeing the forest to see if any guards to the cave made their entrance.

The brave pair waded in a knee-deep stream, bending from the hip slightly as they trudged through the neck of the underground river. The conquering queen had her dagger in one hand, held with bent elbow near her waist and she carried a lit dragon's torch with her other hand so both could see what was underneath them as they progressed ever so slowly because of the crosscurrents; an undertow bit and sucked at their heels while the overcurrent nipped past their kneecaps.

"There must be some sort of tide at that lake," Jacob declared, looking surprised.

"Yes," replied Grace. "It has been a long time, Jacob, but there is a small tide here because … " As she began to remember the area out loud for herself and Jacob's sake, the neck of the cave got somewhat smaller, so the currents got stronger and deeper. Both warriors sheathed their weapons and Jacob took the lantern as Grace was having a hard enough time standing up with both hands on either side of the cave's neck while the water flowed over her thighs. Jacob found himself leaning heavily to one side with his hand almost attached to the neck's wall while he held the lantern with his free hand. They slogged through currents as their feet were sucked in and out of the muddy neck's bed with every step. The straight neck trail led them to a half-closed portal of mud and rock at their thighs with the water flowing over and into it simultaneously.

Jacob told Grace to stop, lean heavily to one side, and hold the torch. She did so. He then fought the overcurrent and pushed and heaved himself through the mud and silt entryway. He found himself facedown in a muddy beach sidestream and still under water. He fought to get up and succeeded. The merchant-mason then braced his feet up against two sturdy sides of stone guarding the entry and bent down to reach his hand and face toward his beloved. All she saw was a hand coming from the top of the hole; she reached to grab it, taking what she thought was a strong step. It wasn't; her one leg slipped on the mucky bottom, but Jacob's grasp was stronger than gravity and he caught her hand to literally pull her up and out of the neck of the cave.

Climbing out of the stream onto what was their left side of the beachhead, they looked beyond them to see the beauty of the cave. Grace had lost the torch; however, they both looked above them, and with the help of fanciful fireflies and other wondrous flying bugs giving off their own light, they marveled at some of the most magnificent stones of all colors glittering with flying light affixed to some beautiful white grotto stone on the walls and ceiling. The air seemed so fresh but as a swoosh of wind suddenly came from the other side of the lake, they smelled sulfur. Looking straight ahead, over the fresh water which was nearly a furlough away, they saw darkness. The glitter in the "skyline" diminished and blackness was a repugnancy across the way that only meant one thing: the dragon and her new lair.

"That 'wind' was the flying dragon, my love," said Grace to Jacob sadly.

The small, melancholy reverberation of an all too familiar voice was all the dragon needed. She swooped down from the ceiling, her glittering wings and body form replicating her high hiding place, now fully noticed but all too late. The totally fatigued travelers had not enough time to unsheathe their swords; Grace was swept up in a moment by vicious claws and carted away like dead carrion.

Although Grace knew her body had been poisoned and paralyzed almost instantaneously by the snake-like venom in the claws, she could still scream out to Jacob, "Wait for the men! Wait for Paul!" She knew her love would try to go it alone, but this would not be enough. *"What if this monster is terribly hungry?"* Grace thought, struck with terror; she did not want her last moment to end as food for her old enemy. Flying through the air, she felt the wind hard on her face but could not move a muscle. "At least I still have my voice and my skin feels the air about me," she desperately mused. "Maybe I can use diplomacy with my embittered adversary." All of a sudden, Grace started to laugh. Why? She knew not. Nonetheless, she could see what she and her enemy shared in common as they approached its side of the lake.

Chapter 18:

Enemies Have Much in Common

Grace felt herself descending, along with the frequent upward draft as the wings bent and heaved because of her extra weight. "My, I guess it does not pay to poison!" shouted the queen to her captor bravely. "I am so much dead weight to you!"

"That you are, mate killer!" shrieked the enemy with a horrible wheeze. Then, out of the blue, Grace heard a tremendous crack and a wing lost its power.

"Oh! My wing bone! Now you've done it, you horrid queen masquerader!" The shriek was now venomous and out of all the breath the poor, wretched creature could have ever had. It let go immediately and Grace fell far, but thank goodness she could not feel a thing when she landed with a thud, first on her feet and then flat on her side on the beach sand. She saw how she had landed but was completely numb. *"I must have dropped a whole house height!"* she thought as absolute fright tried to take her over.

"Love be with me. Forgiveness cover me. Faithland have me once more," she whispered desperately, facing the very scene she had seen from the skies; a sulfuric bonfire of old excrement at a short distance and two dead juvenile monsters recently somehow killed that had started to rot in an area even closer to Grace. The smell and heat almost overwhelmed her with utter nausea. "I can't throw up now," she said out loud to herself. "Hopefully my stomach muscles don't work, either!"

"Hopefully *my* stomach muscles still work even when my bones don't!" hissed the enemy in a wheezy fashion, overhearing her prey. The foul, childless creature had landed in the water and could slither her way up the beachhead.

"Since you are a real believer, you probably won't die of my poison," hissed the dragon, slithering around her prey on the beach. Her belly, bejeweled in the sky, turned as pale white as the cave sand and was very smooth and vulnerable; her back was a chameleonic, chitinous white. The scales could contract upon one another and did when the monster turned and whirled. They also expanded as her whole wormlike body seemed to be able to expand and contract at her brain's command. Her mouth was long, not unlike her body, and the fangs stuck out along with the rest of her teeth from the very hard roof of her upper and even lower jaw. Her mouth, however, was the only thing that did not expand or contract. Even her wings could bend together, not with just two hinges but six or maybe seven; they literally folded into her body.

"Where is your broken bone?" shouted the prey unnervingly.

"Oh! One so paralyzed is worried about my broken bone, is she!" wheezed the dragon. "I cracked it back in place but dare not unfold it ... I can't fly anymore." The lady dragon started to sob uncontrollably. She stopped taunting her dinner and just began to fart and blubber all over her own beach. The sulfurous fumes from her body expulsions and her chemicalized sobs would have been too much for Grace had not a rush of fresh wind come through the dragon vent, along with Paul's men. They came quietly, unnoticed by the weakened female foe. She started her monologue of bitterness without realizing she did not just have an audience of one, but many.

"Do you realize that I can hardly start a fire anymore! I wheeze! I find it hard to breathe. My mate died at your sword, and I have had to bring those wretched brats up all by myself. I'm not a bad mother! It was never my fault that they were left on their own. I had to hunt for my own food. It got harder and harder at Heartland because even remnants of righteousness make it very difficult for a dragon to get its proper food. One starts to feel guilty about eating people who are good souls. I don't know why. It just happens. That wonderful Prince Peter, he was so good; unfortunately, he was also always good with the sword! Even as a youth. That father of his I wouldn't want if my life depended on it; all bad fat and no meat. That is no nourishment for a dragon. So I left. I came here via the neck of the stream and beached myself right under the castle. See my old excrement to the left of the beach here ... yes, about a long alley's way down, the entrance to this cave from the old paymaster's station. I blocked it about a decade ago with sand and my excrement; my children's, too. We were eating well then. There was so much gluttonous greed going on in what was once Faithland. Some were never too fat, though. I guess they desired to keep their figures. Nonetheless, what they wanted to hoard I stole and ate. My children ate from me, much like the birds do. I regurgitated my food when they were very little and, like the birds do, I kicked them out of nest at a very young age. Also, like some birds, we flying dragons mate for life!" The dragon then leered at Grace with her red, swollen eyes and moved her mouth closer to the helpless royal, but was suddenly shocked by her statement.

"My son died as well. And my daughter, well, the only time I really get to see her is when I rescue her from one disaster or another," the fellow single female confessed.

"Do you mean to tell me that the dragon-slayer has an empty nest, too?" said the dragon with a puff of sulfur. Unbeknownst to her, Paul's men were moving in fast behind the dead bodies of the monster's children and the rocks on the beachhead. They made sure to listen to every word.

"The one you left on the other side is my lover, and he has given me two children. One is in heaven and the other is a young lady now," Grace stated without emotion. She would get no sympathy showing weakness but she might get empathy with fact. She was crying tears, but they were reactions to the sulfur and fumes, much like what happens when one peels and cuts very fresh onions. The monster knew that and breathed and puffed in her face to torture her.

Grace started coughing uncontrollably and the monster mocked, "Oh, I'm so terribly sorry. I must stop that. I do not want my dinner to be spoiled with humors of unhappiness."

"The only unhappy one will be you, you fiend!" shouted a warrior as they all suddenly made themselves known in a semicircle surrounding the wicked beast.

Chapter 19:

By Truth, a Truce, and a Monstrous Mother Turns from Fiend to Friend

Her eyes red and swollen, the dragon quickly looked up from her tortured victim's coughs and sneezes with sudden fright; she did try to hide her tremendous fear as, once again, the situation turned against her because of her longtime nemesis. "I was just about to enjoy my precious dinner," she continued with an air of insouciance. "You must admit, gentlemen, your queen isn't much of a meal. Very lean cuisine, very – "

"Quiet your treacherous self!" shouted the lead warrior once again. "Get away from Queen Grace and we will let you live to do yourself a favor."

"Oh," said the dragon, now leaning up on the back of her wormlike tail with one eyebrow up and both eyes looking at the nails on her one claw that had poisoned the queen. "It broke," was all she expressed.

"To save your soft, rotund belly," the warrior remarked as the eyebrow of the dragon stayed up but her eye turned toward the speaker, "you can swim the lake and help us capture the Rogenshire knights who were walking toward the neck of the cave right after our lady and her life partner entered therein. You can do this or die here, right now. I would love to kill you."

"Oh, I'm sure you would," puffed the dragon. Her eye now looked as the other one did, straight ahead at her children's corpses. The warrior saw her destitution and rolled out the truth which, he knew, would at least give her the power to swim the lake and die fighting the enemy. "I heard through the scribe at Rogenshire that the same knights I send you to kill are the same knights who murdered your children as they slept in the public fountain a week ago." He added insult to injury, "Usually that scribe lies through his teeth but this time he was actually telling the truth."

"And how do you know he was telling the truth?" hissed the dragon, turning her whole head away from the queen and looking at the speaker.

"It was that very night that one of the castle servants fled the place never to return, hid behind one of the huge pillars, and saw the whole ungallant act take place," he responded, looking the hideous matron right in the eyes.

"Castle servants tend to lie for their own benefit!" screeched the vexed mother, lowering her head and turning her wormy body toward the warrior. She lost all attention over her prey because of her emotional scar. This was what the man wanted; he continued to speak, backing up as if retreating. In actuality, he was giving himself and the monster more space from Queen Grace, making himself the subject of her fury.

"Sometimes servants do lie, which is unfortunate," agreed the noble fighter. "However, the servant I speak of is my daughter Pricilla, who loves truth and hates lies. She fled – "

The dragon stopped short and interrupted her opponent. Her eyes widened and her jaded self seemed to relax in a joy after one happy moment flashed through her mind. "You mean the charming, beautiful young Pricilla, that selfsame strong young lady who turned a whole supply of sheep going to the king's court back to the peasantry?" The dragon grinned at the thought as only a dragon can, sitting back up on her tail and leaving herself completely at risk. Her claw touched her dagger-like tooth in contemplation.

"She allowed me two sheep that day," mused the monster. "I was so grateful that I could actually talk with her. She was so valiant and unafraid. Courage and right was the only armor she had. I only took what was necessary for me as her family in the peasantry had already given the king his share; he was taking much too much."

"That is the whole point, my friend," feigned the fighter, putting down his sword a bit and hoping for a short truce at least. "The extra sheep were to be given to these same knights who killed your children."

At that statement the dragon wheezed in fury. What would have been a mighty shatter of air by fire was a long, billowy puff of dusty, sulfuric mist. Nonetheless, the dragon's courage and madness were still at full prime, and she turned and slithered past Queen Grace into the water and disappeared.

Chapter 20:

One Final Battle, Two Royal Marriages, and Four Coronations

The other side of the lake was drowning in pools of blood as the dragon slithered her way up the sandy shore. Paul and his men had noticed the cantankerous evil knights coming to drink from the stream just as Grace and Jacob entered therein. These wicked, brawny wretches did not notice Paul and his army, nor did they see the break up to the other side of the forest floor; however, they noticed the queen and her partner and quietly followed them into the neck of the cave. As soon as Grace was taken, Jacob had found himself cornered between the sea and an army of rogue knights. He was about to enter the water, knowing that they might not follow him in nearly full armor. Indeed, his plan did partially work as they began helping each other disrobe the large parts still left on their heavy-plated shells. The rogues left themselves unknowingly much more vulnerable as the forest army descended on them by surprise, having followed them secretly through the neck. By the time the dragon got there, half of her work was done. She could tell the difference between the men because she also admired Paul and could never bring herself to battle him. The rogue knights still had most of their leg gear on which depleted their ability to run swiftly. All Paul and his army had to do was feign retreat and split in half, going west and east along the beach, literally running away as quickly as possible from the semi-crusted group.

Half of the rogues still alive turned to see their other nemesis but it was way too late for them. Somehow, the dragon, being so wretchedly vexed and enraged, spewed out the last amount of fire she possibly could and cooked them all, in and out of their armor. Even their slain on the beachhead were either fried by her fury or roasted in semi-shell. She immediately began her feast while Paul and his warriors slipped from the beach back through the neck and ran to the opposite entrance, which was the dragon's vent. The dear dragon ate way too much and too quickly; after having swum back to her side of the lake she dropped dead of a full stomach and a broken heart.

Grace and the men saw the dragon's approach and watched her die near her slain children on her own beach. "At least her last moment was a pleasant one," said Jacob as he and five other men shouldered Grace, who was on a cloth secured, handmade, wooden flat board. They were able to pulley her up from the vent into the fresh forest air and walk with her toward the palace. The Rogenshire peasantry had had enough of her wicked brother and declared as much by the fountain at the square. There was no wicked knight or squire left in Rogenshire, and Grace, albeit paralyzed, was given her throne back by her own people; Pricilla returned from the forest being at their head.

The wicked brother stood at the balcony of the castle and commenced descending the new spiral staircase attached to it, hand on the sheath of his sword. Paul immediately noticed this and so did Pricilla; they were both wonderfully ready to purge his dust from Grace's presence when they heard a very familiar voice behind them shout, "Hoo, wicked cousin! It is time to fight and defend your sister the queen from your impudence and repugnant abuse!" King Peter unsheathed his sword as he and the hermit approached the fountain on Montgomery from the cobbled street, Montgomery's hooves trumpeting the new king's entrance with goodly foreboding to evil. The hermit alit from the grand stallion, smiling, and made his way to Grace's side. She had been gingerly put down safely on an oak table outside a shop. No one bothered to really take notice of him. All the people winced as King Peter descended from his steed with renewed strength, his newly polished armor glittering in the rays of the sunset. Montgomery's armor reflected his presence so well that the wicked adversary was totally blinded for more than one disadvantaged moment.

Everyone parted to watch the fatal sword fight take place. King Peter took off his helmet as Grace's sore sibling did not have his on. They dueled, but Peter was far too advanced for the poor wretch to handle. One could say that the duel was even boring and lasted but a few brief winks as the ambidextrous iron man with the golden spurs slaughtered an outwitted and out-of-his-prime cowardly abuser in the twinkling of a hermit's eye.

Everyone cheered as the wretch fell near the walls of the fountain. Their cheers turned to shouts and waves of joy as Queen Grace herself walked up to her dead brother, took the signet ring off his pinky finger, placed it on her right forefinger, and held her hand up, praising God with shouts of ecstasy as she kept looking up into the dimming sky with tears streaming down her face. Everyone, including King Peter, joined in the Praise to the Lord, but no one ever knew, except those who knew the hermit, how Grace the Queen was healed.

The hermit had long since disappeared from the fountain area after the praises dimmed with the night. Messengers were sent to the rest of the forest people and to Heartland to announce that Grace was queen and she and King Peter, who was king and still alive, proclaimed that the Lord of love had saved the kingdoms. They also declared a feast for all people at Faithland. Preparations and feasting began shortly after all the people arrived at Grace's estates. Tirzah, Cassandra, and the other maidens were able to celebrate their freedom with everyone else.

Queen Grace, who had been regent, made the decision to share her throne with Jacob, thus making him a king equal to her. They married the same day of their coronation, which was the first day of the celebration; these days were seven in all! Tirzah was given the position of royal advisor to both kingdoms; she was also bestowed the title of Princess Royal and Heiress Apparent to the throne of Faithland.

After a full week of joy, everyone went to Heartland and rejoiced at the marriage of King Peter and one-time commoner, now Queen Cassandra. Their coronation was also the first celebration, and, as before, the rejoicing lasted for seven days! Cassandra's father was given wonderful rooms in the castle in which to reside and, along with Paul and other master tradesmen, he received the title Honorary Member of the Cabinet for both Faithland and Heartland. They answered only to the king and queen therein.

As for the masquerading hermit, He always was and He always will be. There is no end to His *love*. There is no end to His stories, for they are His people and they are wrapped in his mysterious, eternal love.

CPSIA information can be obtained at www.ICGtesting.com
Printed in the USA
LVOW08s1616060813

346577LV00005B/644/P